Letters to Oma

For Hannah ~
I hope you think
"Oma" is _wunderbar_!

Mary Duraseil
1997

Letters to Oma

A young German girl's account of her
first year in Texas,
1847

Marj Gurasich

illustrations by Barbara Mathews Whitehead

A Chaparral Book

TEXAS CHRISTIAN UNIVERSITY PRESS
Fort Worth

Library of Congress Cataloging-in-Publication Data

Gurasich, Marj.
    Letters to Oma : a young German girl's account of her first year
in Texas, 1847 / by Marj Gurasich.
        p.   cm. — (A Chaparral book)
    Summary: After her family moves from Germany to Texas in 1847,
fifteen-year-old Tina chronicles in letters to her grandmother their
struggle to survive in a strange new place while preserving their
traditional German ways.
    ISBN 0-87565-037-6
    [1. German Americans—Fiction.   2. Emigration and immigration—
Fiction.   3. Texas—Fiction.   4. Letters.]   I. Title.
PZ7.G98145Le   1989
[Fic]—dc19   88-38747
                                       CIP
                                       AC

∞

Designed by Whitehead & Whitehead

W

Fifth Printing

The cover illustration is based on a German traditional folk art called *fraktur. Frakturs* were decorated and carefully lettered documents recording births, weddings, awards of merit, and deaths. They often used similar design motifs such as tulips, birds, vines and hearts.

For my sister, Harriett,
who shares with me our German heritage

With grateful thanks to
Valerie Woolvin, Sisterdale
Dr. Stephen Gish, Houston
Sarah Gish, Houston
Stephen Gurasich

Preface

I N the early 1800s Germany consisted of a confederation of thirty-nine states. Many Germans, especially the liberal, free-thinking university students and professors, agitated for German unity and a constitutional government with freedom of speech and trial by jury.

While political unrest fermented in the German states, a single, poorly organized, underpopulated province in the New World was successfuly revolting from its powerful ruler—Mexico. That province was Texas, as of 1836 an independent republic with all the freedoms the German liberals sought.

In 1845 the United States Congress voted to admit Texas to the Union. Officially ratified in 1846, Texas became the twenty-eighth state in the Union and those freedoms were guaranteed to all who would seek them.

The German free-thinkers naturally looked toward Texas as a refuge from oppression and a safe haven for fleeing political activities. Texas was also eyed as a possible German colony by a group of well-intentioned but impractical nobles. They called their organization the Society for the Protection of German Emigrants in Texas, *Adelsverein* or, simply, *Verein*.

The *Verein* promised gifts of land, housing, horses, and farm implements to thousands of Germans who came streaming to the "land of milk and honey," as the *Verein* described Texas.

Totally inexperienced and untrained in business matters, the nobles quickly used up all their funds and in 1847 went bankrupt.

When many of the boat-weary settlers finally arrived at Galveston or the *Verein* port of Indianola, they learned, to their dismay, that no help, no land, nothing awaited them—nothing that is but hardship and back-breaking work, disease and (too often) death. They soon depleted their savings buying land, wagons, and teams of oxen and what few supplies were available.

The disappointed German settlers, in a strange country and without the help they had been promised, nevertheless faced the uncertain future with courage and determination and a strong belief in the value of hard work.

Their descendants, still living in the "German belt" of Texas, attest to the success of their efforts to found a colony of "free men in a free land."

Letters to Oma

TINA stood shivering in the cold hallway of their *Fach- werk* home in Varel, Oldenburg, as she listened to excited voices urging her father to get away.

"It is not safe for you here, Max."

"Who knows when they might come for you?"

"You are a marked man, Max. You must leave right away, *ja*."

Papa had written papers at the University, papers condemning the government and urging the people to demand a democracy for Germany. These friends had come to warn him that the police were going to arrest him and that he should flee for his life.

"But where, where do I take my loved ones?" he asked quietly.

He was not one to raise his voice. Mama could handle that part. Tina always wished her mother were more like Oma, Grandmother Lembke, who, although she was Mama's own mother, was so different.

"Christina Eudora von Scholl, you are just like my mother," Mama said whenever Tina irritated her. "You two would live with your heads in a book and your ears tuned for hearing faeries in the forest."

Mama set her thin lips even thinner and went about her baking or sewing or cleaning. And Oma Lembke and her look-alike granddaughter, Christina, glanced at one another, the faded blue eyes of the elder crinkling at the smiling bright-with-youth blue eyes of the younger. Yes, Mama was right; they *were* alike, she and Oma. Both had fine, mobile features in their heart-shaped faces. Only she was tall and slender, while Oma was so tiny she looked like a wind would blow her away. Tina thought how much she loved her little grandmother.

Papa and the men in the study were still discussing the fate of her family.

"The *Adelsverein* will help you, Max," said Papa's old friend, Heinrich Voelker. "These noblemen have a *wunderbar* plan to form a German colony in the new American state they call Texas. I read a letter from Friedrich Ernst who used to live here in Oldenburg. He has founded a town called Industry in this Texas. He says it is beautiful and that great opportunity for a good life awaits anyone willing to work. But, most important," Herr Voelker's voice rose as he spoke with emotion, "Texas means freedom for you and your family, Max, *freedom!*"

The talk went on for many hours, to the clink of beer steins, as the men, most of them professor friends of Papa's, begged him to leave the country for his own safety.

Tina crept up to her room in the old two-story house and climbed into the high four-poster walnut bed which had been built for Great-great-grandmother von Scholl. She thought about what the men downstairs were saying. Would she have to leave her precious bed and the home of her ancestors? Her school friends and the music society she loved? And, what about Oma?

Tina knew about Oma's sickness. She had faced the fact, when Mama explained in her matter-of-fact way, "Christina, your grandmother will not live much longer. She dies a little each day. You must help her to be happy in her last months."

Tina had swallowed her tears and tried to force her lips into a tight line like Mama's to keep from screaming, "No, no! Not Oma!"

The tears came later, in this very bed, her head buried in the soft goosedown pillow. And now downstairs, they talked of sailing vessels and seaports and Texas; of vast lands and wide open skies and freedom. Ordinarily, Tina would have been enraptured by this talk for she was naturally an adventurous person. Now she could only think, "What of Oma?"

She knew they would have to leave her grandmother behind with Uncle Heinrich and Aunt Rosa. And she would never see her little, sprightly, chirpy grandmother again.

As the tears came Tina whispered a prayer for Oma, "Dear God, take care of my grandma. Her laughter will make heaven a happier place. But, please, not yet."

And then one for herself, "Heavenly Father, please make me strong like Mama and wise and kind like Papa. But, even more, give me a happy heart like my little Oma's, because she is *me* then, and I am *her* now.

"Amen."

For the next few weeks the family sorted and packed their belongings, Papa lingering over each book as he decided which to take and which to give to the village school library.

"How slow you go, Max, we will never leave Germany!" Mama scolded. Once Papa had explained the danger of staying in Germany and that they would find freedom in Texas, Mama quit objecting to the move and threw herself into the preparations, taking everyone along in her path.

The little boys argued over whether Wilhelm's lead soldiers or Fritz' toy mechanical banks should go. Mama had allowed one big crate for their things, and it was full already.

"How can we leave these things, Mama?" Fritz asked with tears in his eyes. "Wilhelm says we won't ever come back home. Is it true, what Wilhelm says?"

"Stop crying, now, and pack. Each one put half of your

treasures into the chest, and then ask Papa to nail it shut. One more done now." Mama was getting impatient.

Tina went about her packing with quiet efficiency. She had a heavy weight in her chest; better not try to talk with it there. When Oma came downstairs for her afternoon *Schnapps*, perhaps she would feel better. Perhaps.

Mama's lovely Bavarian china and pewter tea and coffee set were carefully packed in wooden boxes and set beside the old black walnut dining table. Tina looked at its beautifully turned legs and deep, intricate carving, the surface still lustrous though many generations had sat around it in the high backed chairs with their padded covers made from old tapestries.

"I will not live like a heathen," Mama declared for one and all to hear. "We do not need to be uncivilized, just because we go to an uncivilized country. We will have our silver and fine linens and all the things we need to keep a decent house in that distant country of Texas. It cannot be otherwise."

Tina gathered her few treasures, a necklace with a fine silver filigree cross that Papa had brought her from Italy; a doll with china head and glass eyes that somehow the boys had not broken. She would take it to help her remember her childhood. She would take some favorite books and her collection of friendship cards signed by her classmates at school. How she would miss Berthe and Lisette and, yes, even Johann who always teased her. She picked up one of the cards, with its ornate design of hearts and roses entwined, and read the words,

Das beste Glück sei dir beschieden,
So wandle froh durchs Leben hin;
In deinem Herzen wohne Frieden,
Auch sei für mich ein Plätzchen drin.

May happiness to you be given,
So go through life joyously;
May peace reside within your heart,
And may there be a little place for me.

As she fought back the tears that welled unbidden, in her eyes, she heard Oma's voice calling her from the library.

"Tina, I have brought you something special to take to the new land—to keep always fresh the memory of your old Grandma!"

Tina ran into the library, her long, straight brown hair flying behind her, not really seeing the dark, gleaming paneled walls or the worn, richly colored patterned rugs rolled up on the parquet floor. She did not notice the empty shelves where her father's favorite books had resided for so many years; or the great stone fireplace, stretched across one entire wall, where the family had roasted chestnuts and warmed cider when the snows came. She saw only her grandmother, Oma, whom they would soon leave behind, probably never to see again.

The old lady sat in one of the two deep red leather chairs, high backed to ward off drafts in the cold German winters, her feet not quite touching the floor. She looked tinier than ever, Tina thought, as though she had shrunk since she heard the news of their leaving. But Oma held her head high and her steady eyes watched Tina closely to catch each change of the girl's expression.

"For you, my dear," Oma said, holding out her arms to Tina. In her hands she held the most exquisitely carved wooden clock Tina had ever seen. Its warm dark wood was shaped into vines intertwined with flowers and leaves of ivy, carved with the finest craftsmanship.

"Many years ago, when he was a young man, your Grandfather Lembke worked for a clockmaker. He made this little clock for me. It is my dearest possession, packed away these many years.

"See, Christina," her grandmother turned the clock so that Tina could watch. As she moved the hands to the hour, a little door above the clock face opened and a tiny, precious bird bobbed out. "Cuckoo, cuckoo," it chirped. Two o'clock. And back into its home it went, inside the dark interior of the lovely, delicate clock.

5

Tina was entranced. She had never seen such a beautiful clock.

"Oh, Grandma, is it mine? To keep?"

"*Ja, Liebchen,* I want you to keep this little clock with you always to remind you of your little Oma. Do not forget me, my Christina." She stood up, slowly, and turned to leave the room.

"Oh, Grandmama, thank you, thank you. I will cherish it forever. It will never leave me; for what could I love more? It is so beautiful. And it will be an hourly message from you to me."

Tina hugged Oma and kissed her soft, wrinkled cheek. Tina's lips tasted salty from Oma's dried tears. But Oma would never admit to those tears. She tottered slightly and left the room without looking back.

Houston, State of Texas
United States of America
January 5, 1847

Dear, dear Oma,

You must be ever so worried, my dearest Grandmother, since we left you nearly four months ago in Germany and you have heard no news of us.

First of all, let me say that we are all as well as could be expected, and grateful to be alive! Mama and Papa, Wilhelm, Fritz and I have survived an ordeal worse than I ever dreamed we would undergo.

You remember, as we parted, how I could not hold back the tears, for leaving you and our home, and for fear of the future in the far-away, strange place called Texas. Mama was cross with me, and I know that I was no good example for the smaller brothers. I, Christina Eudora von Scholl, a nearly grown woman of fifteen years, was ashamed but could not help myself. I not only hated leaving my beloved homeland, but also feared going to a foreign place where the savages might kill us, one and all.

We have seen no savages yet, but since the hardships we have passed through, I almost would welcome meeting some of these

Indians. Nothing, I think, could be worse than the past few months.

First, Oma, the ship was so overcrowded that Mama and I were cramped with six others into a tiny cabin. Papa and the boys slept in bunks high up near the ceiling between decks. The food was miserable (but how I wished for some of that poor fare later when there was none at all!).

Many passengers became very sick, some dying. We went to the funerals, where bodies were given to the sea, of people we had come to know quite well. Several were little babies, and Wilhelm and Fritz and I stood crying for them.

I will never forget the ocean voyage. The "Neptune" was our unhappy home for fifty-eight days. I began to think we would never set foot on land again. The cold, wet winds chilled our bones and rocked the ship to and fro like a paper boat on a windy pond. Papa, poor Papa, was very seasick and could eat nothing for days and days.

Mama did not allow herself to get sick and so managed to nurse Papa and keep Wilhelm and Fritz busy with their lessons.

"Boys must learn," she said. "There is no time to waste. You, Wilhelm, already ten years old and not doing sums too gut yet. Fritz, six-year-old boys must read better."

They both ducked their heads in shame and studied harder.

To keep my mind busy, after his seasickness passed, Papa helped me with my Latin verbs and started teaching me some English.

"You will need to communicate with the Amerikaners in the New World," he told me.

My fingers I kept warm by spending my days knitting. I had the lovely gray wool you gave me and I knit all of it into stockings for the boys and Papa. They will need them in Texas when the northers come in.

The norther is a strange thing that happens, we are told, in Texas. We met a kindly gentleman on the "Neptune" who is returning to Texas after going home to Germany to ask for money from the Adelsverein. He told us of the northers. Some days will be eighty-five degrees Fahrenheit and very summerlike and, *suddenly, before you can fetch a shawl, the norther swoops in and temperature drops, maybe as much as thirty or forty degrees—always with a wind that chills to the bone, and, sometimes, rain which turns to ice as it comes down.*

Of course, it is winter now here in Texas but today, very pleasant, seventy degrees and blue, blue sky.

But I am getting too far ahead in my story for you. . . . We were tired and hungry and cold on the ship and as we approached the Texas Coast, our captain, Herr Schumann, *told Papa we were lacking in fresh water supply. So he put in at Galveston, a seaport of over five thousand people, the largest city in Texas. All we saw of it was a group of weathered, gray cypress warehouses along the waterfront between Main Street and the shoreline.*

The captain bought supplies for the ship, as well as water and fresh meat. We had tasted no meat for two weeks.

This meat was as tough as shoe leather, Oma. Mama said that they butcher at night and cook it next day which is sure to make it tough. Captain Schumann told Papa that beef costs the settlers five cents a pound, although he could get it cheaper for the ship.

Mama said that was far too dear for such stringy stuff. But Wilhelm said he liked having to chew so hard.

"It makes me know that I am finally eating something," he said.

Little Fritz kept chewing and chewing and finally spat it out. Mama was cross with him, but Papa said, "No matter, he got the juices out of it. He will have the nourishment."

It was good to have even this tough meat after eating nothing but hard biscuits and thin gruel for the last two weeks of our voyage.

Papa and some of the other men decided to charter a steamboat to take us up the Buffalo Bayou to Houston. From there we could go overland to San Felipe and thence to Industry where there were other German settlers. They told the captain they could tolerate conditions aboard the "Neptune" no longer. Papa rented space in a warehouse in Galveston to store all our furniture and most of the household goods temporarily, and we left the ship.

After being on the schooner for fifty-eight miserable days, we were happy to learn that the steamboat took only twelve hours to reach the town of Houston. Also, the food was better and everyone was excited to get nearer and nearer our destination and eager to see what the Verein *had ready for us. . . .*

Now Christina Eudora von Scholl was in this strange country of Texas; a new land, newer than the furniture Mama had insisted on bringing, newer than her own precious clock.

There was something frightening, and fascinating too, about the newness of this place called Texas. Life would never be the same for her or her family as it was in the comfortable, old world of Germany. She must learn the new ways and face the dangers of the new life, but she mustn't forget the old. Especially her dear Oma.

She vowed then, no matter what hardships or dangers might await them, she would never, *never* part with Oma's last gift to her.

I NDUSTRY, Texas
March 17, 1847

Dear Oma,

Although I promised to write you once every month, it has been impossible to do so. The situation for our family has been such the past six weeks as not to know if we would survive at all. But survive it we did, and we finally have come to our new home in the town called Industry.

After my letter from Houston (which I put on a packet the last day of January, so I hope you may receive it soon) our first plan was to go immediately to Industry. Papa planned to meet **Herr Friedrich Ernst,** *the man who wrote the letter about Texas to the newspaper in Oldenburg. It was his letter which Papa read and then decided we would come to Texas, remember?* **Herr Ernst** *founded the town of Industry, the first German settlement in Texas, so Papa would go nowhere else to live.*

Before we could go we must see the **Adelsverein,** *or as it is called here, the* **Verein,** *and get our land and make arrangements for them to build our house. Mama, who had been silent for most of the trip to Houston, doubted the stories we had heard of this heroic society.*

"The **Verein!!** *Ach du lieber! The* **Verein,** *they promise this, they promise that! Three hundred twenty acres of land and a log house and tools and seeds for farming! How do you know they will do what they say? What if you have brought us to this place that God has forsaken for* nichts? *What will become of us?"*

Oma, I tried to sympathize with Mama, but it was hard to do so. Mama always expects so much sympathy, you sort of hold it back. Papa, poor dear Papa, is different. He never asks for anything, never complains, but somehow you always feel sorriest for him. He is carrying an extra heavy burden now, Oma, for it is because of him that we are here.

Mama, in all her worry, was right. The Verein *did not keep its promises. The only land to be had was far, far away in Comanche territory. (Comanches are very war-like Indians!)*

There were no log homes or the materials with which to build them; no plows or oxen; nor any transportation; nothing, not even seed for the crops. The Verein, *it seems, had nearly run out of money and hundreds who came here were left on their own. Many people, sick and dying of the fever, waited for the wagons to take them inland, wagons that never came or came too late.*

Mama was beside herself. She stormed at poor Papa who really was not to blame. But I shouldn't say anything against Mama, should I, Oma? I do not mean to be disrespectful, but I hated to see Mama so angry for something Papa could not help.

"Ach, Max," she moaned, "what do we do now, after all that Verein *foolishness? We have nothing with which to start our new life in this terrible, wild place. What do you intend to do about it?"*

Mama's anger and disappointment made the boys and me so unhappy that we walked away and waited for the storm to cease. We hated to see the look of hurt and sorrow in Papa's eyes, but this time we felt sorry for Mama, too. And ourselves, as well.

Papa talked to some of the other settlers who had been on the boat with us and they decided to pool their monies. They would buy a wagon and team of oxen, then hire a driver to take us all to Industry.

We had to leave behind a crate of Mama's most prized dishes which she had not put in storage for fear of theft or breakage. Now they had to be abandoned because there was no space for them. This upset her even more. I hid the box containing my precious clock within the folds of my cape and no one noticed.

The trip began well, with the women in sunbonnets which they had purchased in Houston (everyone seemed to be wearing them, so they must have them too) riding in the wagon. We children walked alongside. Most of the men rode horses. Papa's horse was a beautiful sorrel for which he had traded his gold watch and which came with saddle and bridle. He named the mare, Schatzie.

"She is a little sweetheart," he said. Papa was trying hard to be happy and optimistic for all our sakes.

We had not gone far when the mosquitoes attacked us. They were huge, and when they bit us, great welts came up that itched and itched. The boys cried all night long and could not sleep. One little girl, Clara, became very sick from the mosquito bites.

The first night, after we had traveled nine miles perhaps to Piney Point or a little beyond, one of the wagon wheels broke. As there were no trees on the prairie, there was no wood to fix the wheel. The driver, a Texian named Jeff who comes from a farm near Industry, finally rode to the nearest settler's place and bought a wheel from a Mr. Baker's wagon to put on ours.

By now it is the second day and the men try to shoot some game (all but Papa who does not own a gun or know how to shoot one), but there is none that they can find, so we eat some strange kind of bread made of corn meal and fried in pork grease in a skillet over an open flame.

I could not help but look at Mama and wonder how, in this wilderness, she would ever get to use all the beautiful things that were so important to her. She must have been thinking the same thing, for she suddenly looked up and caught my eye and smiled a little, sad smile. I think I felt closer to Mama in that moment than I ever have in my whole life, Oma. But a minute later she was fussing at Papa again about the delay and about the manners of our Amerikaner driver who spat into the fire, much to Mama's disgust!

By the third day, several people (there were sixteen in the party) had fallen ill with fever and Mama made Wilhelm, Fritz, and me stay away from everyone for fear we would come down with it. Sad to say, Oma, four, no—five died within the next two weeks on that gruesome trip. We stopped each time to bury them

and leave their graves marked with wooden crosses. One man,
Herr Schmidt, was a woodcarver; he carved their names and the
date on the crosses.

The little girl, Clara, was the first one who died. She was only
four years old, and her mama and papa wept and wept over her
little grave. Herr Schmidt carved a short verse on her cross.
It read,

> Es war ein unschuldig's Kindlein,
> Dieses Friedhofs Grundstein.
>
> *This innocent child, so dear,*
> *Was the first one buried here.*

Our troubles were not over, Oma. Sometimes it was so very
hot and damp that our clothes clung to our skins. Then the
norther (which I talked of in my first letter, remember?) would
swoop down, and we would be pinched and bitten by cold winds
and rain. Many more became sick and Mama and the other
women were kept busy nursing them and feeding the hungry
with what means they had. Mama finallly let me help, and I tried
to remember all the things you taught me about herbs and healing
plants. However, I could find only chamomile and dandelion and
could not identify the strange ones here.

The worst thing that happened was when the wagon bogged
down in the Brazos River . . . .

Tina was riding in the wagon when the accident happened. She had been tending the sick all night, and Mama
told her to get into the wagon to rest. The boys were cud-
dled up beside her.

When they reached the fast-moving river with steep,
wooded banks on both sides, Jeff motioned for everyone
to get out of the wagon to lighten the load. The sick ones
would be carried across on the backs of the horses.

"Let the children stay; they are light and they need
rest," commanded Mama. Jeff, although not understanding her words, nevertheless interpreted quite well her
tone of voice and her gestures. He grinned and shrugged.

Suddenly a lurch and splash, and the wagon tipped and tilted dangerously close to going over. The cold, muddy-red waters of the river came rushing in before Tina and the boys even realized what had happened.

"*Ach*, Mama! Papa!" cried Wilhelm. Fritz grabbed Tina to keep from falling out of the now far-listing wagon. Tina snatched at the two boys and held on tightly as she heard the shouts of the men and the screams of the women.

Her eyes frantically searched the contents of the wagon. She saw the box she was looking for, high on the stack of trunks behind her. Quickly she told Wilhelm to hold tight around her waist and, with her free arm, reached out and rescued her little clock.

She tied the corners of her wool paisley shawl securely around the box. Then she fastened it to the highest rib of the wagon top.

"Cut the oxen loose, before they git pulled under and drown," yelled Jeff, who had been thrown into the rushing water when the wagon went over. Papa, who was the only one who understood English, plunged into the water and headed for the wagon.

"The children, first, the children!" Mama's voice was hoarse with fear.

With a last worried glance at her clock hanging in the top of the wrecked wagon, tied up like a Christmas present in her pretty scarf, Tina pushed her brothers in front of her and, standing on the rim of the wagon cover, jumped into the cold water. She knew the boys could swim; they always swam in the river behind their home in Oldenburg. "Like fish, those boys," Mama used to say with pride. She did not much approve of Christina swimming, though. It was not ladylike. As for Tina, she was mightily glad now that she was a good strong swimmer, for the current was very swift, and little Fritz could not fight against it too long.

She grabbed his collar and pulled him behind her as she watched Wilhelm swimming ahead and struggling onto the muddy bank. He turned to help her with Fritz just as

Papa came climbing up out of the water. Papa reached for Tina's hand and pulled her up, Fritz dragging behind like a wet sack of potatoes.

"My little Tina, you are a woman grown, with a strong body and a quick mind. You have saved your brothers' lives this day."

Papa's gray-blue eyes clouded with an emotion he seldom displayed. As they walked back toward Mama and the others, he scrubbed his nose with his coat sleeve. Tina could not help but smile; he looked so like little Fritz when he would do the same thing—with Mama fussing at him all the while.

Mama was not fussing now. She was white as a ghost and ran to the boys, gathering them to her bosom, folding her long woolen skirt around them to shield them from the cold wind. Tina watched for a moment and then hurried over where the other people were huddled, trying to decide what to do.

The teamster, Jeff, was saying, "Wall, there's nothin' to do but go get another wagon for these h'yer oxen and leave that one behind." Her father translated Jeff's Texian speech as well as he could and nodded in agreement. *Herr* Oberg offered to go with Jeff to pay for the wagon. The cost would be divided among them all when they returned.

This meant camping out while waiting. No one knew what to expect in these thick woods along the river bottom. Were there wild animals around or, worse, Indians? They knew little of living off the land. So they gathered firewood in silence and fear, built a fire near the river bank and sat before it in despair, waiting for the worst to happen.

Some of the older boys wanted to go look for game, but their mothers would have none of it; so it was cornbread again for supper. Mama and the other women quickly had learned how to make this Texas staple because it looked like that would be all they might have to eat for a long

time, until they could get a crop in. How they missed their white potatoes and wheat bread!

These Texas people did not eat right. All they ate was sweet potatoes and this everlasting corn bread. It wouldn't be too bad if they would mix a little wheat flour with it and let it rise with a sourdough starter; then it would taste like something and would not be hard as a rock the next day like this worthless stuff.

As Mama was expressing her dissatisfaction with food in Texas, one of the women defended the Texans. She had talked earlier with a Texas woman who spoke a little German. She said that flour cost six dollars a barrel and an additional three dollars for transportation, but "corn is grown and ground right here for very little. So the Texans make do with what they can afford."

Mama sniffed at that, because she thought the *Amerikaners* a bit lazy, not bothering with gardens and fresh vegetables and such.

With all the talk of food, Tina's stomach twisted in hunger. The cornbread was too hot to eat yet, so she sat and daydreamed in her wet, muddy clothes, with her hair stringy and teeth chattering. She thought of the homeland, and how lovely it was in the spring, and how good Oma's dumplings were, and *Strudel* and *Sauerbraten*!

"Come, eat, Christina," Mama called sharply. "You must have nourishment, such as it is. Then, out of those wet clothes. I will wash them and hang them on the bushes to dry while you sit by the fire wrapped in the blanket I found that did not get drowned!"

Tina's eyes lit up, not at the thought of the food she so needed, but at Mama's concern for her comfort. She needed that even more than the Texas cornbread.

It was three days before Jeff got back with another wagon and an additional team of oxen. Papa and the others had to divide *Herr* Oberg's cost, $150 for the wagon, $35 for the team of oxen.

After salvaging what they could by swimming out to the wagon and pulling things off, they still had to leave much luggage behind. They found Tina's clock safe and dry, still hanging from the wagon rim, her scarf tied securely around it. Tina sighed with relief.

"I seem to be leaving a trail behind me," Mama grumbled. She still was not reconciled to the loss of her beloved china, and now, all her best dresses and bonnets were in one of the abandoned chests. What next?

. . . What happened next, Oma, was more frightening than falling in the river. Indians!

We were progressing well with the new wagon and the double team of oxen and would soon reach our destination when we saw Jeff suddenly reach for his gun behind him. He stealthily pulled it around next to his right hand which rested idly on the seat. He did not look to right or left. Suddenly the bushes in front of the wagon parted, and there were two savages on ponies staring at us.

I heard Mama and some of the ladies gasp, and I must confess I felt my heart go thump! in my chest. The Indians wore almost no clothing, Oma (a disgrace, Mama said later), and they had beads around their necks and a feather or two stuck in their shiny, black hair. They are not "redskins," as people call them; their skin is tawny brown. They have high cheekbones and a regal way about them—as though they own the place (Papa says they do—they were here first, after all!).

No one said a word. Then they rode up to Wilhelm and Fritz and got down off their horses. Mama gave a little shriek and started toward them, but the first one put his hand up in a most imperious manner and Mama stopped still, the first time I have ever seen anyone get the better of Mama. The taller Indian walked over to Fritz and reached out and touched his flaxen hair. The other did the same to Wilhelm. We were paralyzed with fear for we had been told stories of Indians kidnapping settlers' children, or worse, killing and scalping them.

With a strange look about him, Papa started toward the Indians, like a Christian might have looked going into the lions' den. The Indian who was nearest Papa took a step towards him. His right hand held a knife, its blade a flash of silver with the midday sunshine catching it; his left hand pushed poor Fritz along ahead of him. I was so frightened for him, I could not breathe.

"Boy good," the Indian said, straining to make himself understood. "White hair good. Swap! Swap!" He motioned to his friend who came forward with two large hams.

That was the last straw for Mama; she swooped down on those Indians, telling them what she thought of people who would offer to "swap" hams for boys! I was sure they would scalp her at once, but, instead, they started to laugh and laugh!

Papa thought this a fine chance to end the affair in a friendly manner. So he pulled off his solid gold ring which his university friends had presented him when we left Germany (you remember it, Oma?) and solemnly showed it to the Indian who seemed to be the leader.

Papa pointed to the hams, then to the ring. "Swap," he said with a steady, firm voice. The Indian took the ring, examined it carefully and put the hams in Papa's outstretched hands.

"Swap!" he said, grinning.

Papa gently pulled the boys away from where the two Indians stood. The savages turned on their heels and mounted their ponies and rode off without another word. I can tell you, Oma, that every one of us let out a sigh of relief. Even Jeff, who had kept his hand on his rifle all the while, looked mighty happy.

As we rode along, reliving the frightening adventure, it somehow became funnier and funnier in the retelling. We started to sing some of the old songs of the homeland.

We had been together for a long time now, in all sorts of happenings, and our trip was about over. Of the sixteen who had started this hard journey together, only nine remained. The path along the way was marked with Herr Schmidt's crosses. But in a few hours we would see the first signs of Industry, State of Texas, United States of America. Our hearts were grateful to God that, difficult though the journey had been, we had come through it to find our new life in a new land.

And this, my gentle Oma, is how we arrived at our new home, far from our fatherland and far from you. I could only hope it was for a good future that we had come so far.

Mama is calling, I must go. I will tell you of our home and our new life next time.

Your loving Granddaughter,
Christina Eudora von Scholl

21

I NDUSTRY, Texas
April 25, 1847

Dear Oma,

The first thing I must tell you is that when we were here but two days a wagon came in from Houston with some settlers and also with two letters from you! We just missed the packet when we left there, but as good fortune would have it, these people were right behind us and brought all the mail with them. It was the happiest thing to see your sweet, small script on that envelope. We all sat down on a fallen log on the side of the road, and Papa read the letters to us. I am glad that you are feeling better and hope you will continue going to the doctor you speak of so highly.

We miss you, too, and I think of you each and every day with a little sadness in my heart.

It has been a busy time for us. In the past month, much has happened. First of all, when we arrived here we went immediately to the hotel of Herr Friedrich Ernst, the founder of this town. He and his wife, Louise, have a two-story frame hotel, and many who come here stay at their place until they can build their own house or decide to move on.

Papa and Herr Ernst have much in common. Both are from Oldenburg and both enjoy music and gardening. Herr Ernst was a gardener at the castle in the village, but Papa, always busy in the university, had never before met him.

It is a good thing that Herr Ernst is so trained, and our friend, because he knows what things to plant in a garden and how to make the most of the soil. Papa will have much to learn from him. This is all new to poor Papa, and I feel he is much confused.

Mama is waiting for the wagons with her precious belongings to arrive from Galveston. Papa had arranged for them to follow us in two weeks. We have heard nothing, and Mama is beginning to fuss about it.

The boys and I have been looking around this new land and getting acquainted with the other children here. Wilhelm has found a friend, Hans, who likes to fish and swim as much as he does. Fritz is a little shy and stays close to Mama except when I take him with me to walk around Industry.

This is a strange little village, nothing like our villages at home, Oma. So primitive it is, log cabins for houses and dirt streets. Even (I know you will not believe this) many houses have dirt floors!

Mama is horrified, but Papa says it will not always be so and that, in a few years, we will not even remember the hardships of today.

One piece of good news, Oma. There is a post office, a real one, here in Industry. We are told it is the second one in the state of Texas.

Herr *Seiper, son-in-law of* **Herr** *Ernst, is Postmaster in the small building built of native stone. He says that you may address your letters to us, "General Delivery, Industry, Texas, United States of America." It should not take so long to get your letters now.*

The land around Industry is a pleasant, rolling grassland with pecan, ash and oak trees dripping a strange, ghost-like gray moss they call Spanish moss. It gives the woods an eerie look, especially when ground fog comes rolling in and floats just above the grass. The boys are sure it is ghosts we see. Papa reassures them that it is just the change in temperature from day to night that causes it to happen. They are not positive that Papa is right about the ground fog.

Papa has hired Jeff to stay with us and help us build our home. I am glad. Jeff is seventeen and last year came with his family from a state in America called Tennessee.

Jeff is tall and skinny, with red hair and many freckles. He is also very strong and has cut down many trees and fashioned one large room for our temporary home. It was slow, hard work, even with Papa doing whatever he could, but Jeff never seems to get tired. Even after working from five in the morning until sunset, with only some fried cornmeal bread dipped in (ugh!) molasses for lunch, he still has time to help Mama and me hoe the small garden plot. Mama would not rest until she had started her garden.

The land which Papa purchased from another settler (whose family had been wiped out by the fever) is beautiful. The soil is black and rich and should be very good for vegetables and corn. They do not raise wheat here. **Herr Ernst** *raises cotton and tobacco, though, and is doing very well sending his cigars to New Braunfels for selling to the prosperous farmers there.*

Prince Carl von Solms-Braunfels was the head of the **Verein** *when it first brought people here from Germany and he founded the city of New Braunfels. They say he meant well but was not much help to the settlers and very high and mighty, not at all like Baron Ottfried Hans von Meusebach who heads the* **Verein** *now. He immediately changed his name to plain John O. Meusebach, and he works as hard as anyone else. We have not met him, although Papa would like to someday, because all have good to say about him.*

We have 240 acres of rich, black soil just outside of Industry. Papa had to pay one dollar per acre for it; Mama almost collapsed when she found out how much he had spent.

"We will be penniless soon, Max," she complained. The trip had cost us dearly, with Papa's share of the steamboat trip and all the expense of the two wagons and such.

"All our savings will be gone, then what will we do?"

Papa, as usual, stooped a bit under Mama's scorching tongue and pulled on the moustache he has grown since we left home. (The boys and I think it very distinguished, but Mama does not much like it, the moustache.)

"Emilie," he said with a sad little smile, "I do the best I can. We will survive. You will see. It will be better when your precious things arrive from Galveston; then you will not be so homesick as now."

"Ach, Max," Mama looked at Papa as though to say something more, then just turned and started working very hard

again on the boys' clothes she was mending. Their clothes were in tatters from the long voyage and wagon ride, and Mama would not let them go around looking like those Amerikaners *she saw in town.*

"They go in rags, looking like ruffians. I will not have you go such. We can be clean and mended and act like civil people, even here in this God-forsaken place."

It is clear Mama does not think much of Texas. The boys and I hope that she will change her mind, since we think it is a wunderbar *place and cannot wait to become Americans in every way. I am learning English from Papa, although we say nothing to Mama about it; she would not like it. She refuses to think of this place as anything but an extension of her homeland and a part of Germany, even though it is so "uncivilized."*

Christina put down her mending and looked at the blue sky of Texas. She felt a deep, happy excitement inside for the first time since she had left Oldenburg. She knew that she had "come home" to this new, free land.

She loved the green, rolling hills around Industry with their scattered trees. The cattle of the settlers who had been here for awhile roamed freely and fed on the thick tufts of mesquite grass.

The wild flowers strewn across the hillsides for the past month had been more beautiful than anything Tina had ever seen—vivid orange Indian paintbrush, pink buttercups. ("Why *butter*cups when they are pink, not yellow?" demanded Fritz.)

Her favorite was a lupin-like flower that bloomed in vast sheets of color; solid fields of bright, cobalt blue took your very breath away when you looked at them. They were called bluebonnets, and Tina knew she would never see another flower she would love as much. To her, they symbolized her new life in Texas. They grew everywhere, coming up unbidden and untended, but dauntless, filling the air with their spicy fragrance. Nothing could stop them; they were a part of Texas.

She would be like that, she thought; no matter what she had to do to help her family survive these early hardships, they would learn to love this land and become a part of it, like the bluebonnets.

She told no one of her feelings. Oma was the only one who would have understood, but she was far away. Papa might feel the same way about their new homeland, but she had never talked about her feelings with Papa. Now he was so distracted with his responsibilities, he had no time for her girlish nonsense.

Tina had not much time for thought, either, as she kept very busy during this waiting time. Mama saw to that.

After all the clothes were put in order and washed in the river (a job none of them had ever done before), they must gather wild blackberries which grew everywhere and were ripening fast in the warm April sunshine.

"Take a stick with you," warned *Frau* Ernst. "You must watch for snakes."

Tina shuddered. What would she do if she were to come face to face with a snake? The boys grinned and said they hoped to meet an old snake and they would take care of it fast enough.

When they gathered the berries, they ate and ate this first fruit they had seen since leaving home.

"*Ach,*" Mama said, finally. "Stop, you will be breaking out in the hives, from so much berries! Go get water from the river, and I will boil some of them for jelly, if *Frau* Ernst has some sugar to spare."

A little of the precious coarse sugar was meted out for the jelly. Most of it *Frau* Ernst was saving for making wine when the wild mustang grapes would ripen in July.

Mama, of course, was in her glory to be in a real kitchen again and could not say enough for all the conveniences *Frau* Ernst had in hers.

"Your stove is very good, *Frau* Ernst," she said, smiling at her hostess. "It is good the way each opening can be covered to cook on and how you can control the heat somewhat. Much better than cooking in a fireplace or, as we have been doing, over an open flame outdoors.

"I will be glad when my stove arrives from its storage place in Galveston. I cannot understand where it can be."

Tina also longed for their things to arrive from Galveston. She was homesick for her keepsakes and for her own books, although she was allowed to read *Herr* Ernst's books when her chores were done.

If she had not had her little Oma's clock, she would have been lonesome. It ticked merrily away and sang its cuckoo song and kept her from being too sad when the quiet evening moments came and she thought of the grandmother she had left behind.

There was little time for brooding, though. Tina was learning to help Jeff with the construction of their little log house. Soon it would be done and they would have a place of their own again.

Jeff, with Tina watching admiringly, cut down trees about four inches thick and cunningly put them together without any nails so they formed the walls. By cutting notches in the ends of the logs and fitting them into each other around and around the house, Jeff made the walls grow. He cut openings for doors and windows and made the roof from logs split in half and fitted together in the same way.

"Nails are a might too hard to come by," Jeff explained to Tina, who could just barely understand what he was saying. Jeff's English did not match the English Papa was teaching her, but somehow she got his meaning when they talked.

When Papa brought Mama out to the property to see their house for the first time, she looked as though she might faint. Her face turned pale, and she looked from Jeff to Tina to Papa. All of them wore proud, pleased expressions on their faces.

"What do you think, Emilie?" Papa turned to look at his wife. He knew, when he saw her face, what she was thinking. His own face fell, waiting for the shower of harsh words he knew was coming.

"*Ach*, Max," Mama sighed. "It is a fine house. We will make a home of it someday."

Everyone was so relieved at Mama's reaction, they laughed out loud and started to sing. Mama joined in, though Tina knew what an effort her mother had just made. Her heart went out to her mother, and once again, she thought of her as a woman with wants and desires of her own.

She is not even really so old, Tina thought. Mama must be thirty-two or thirty-three, I think. It is her tight face and the tight-drawn way she combs her hair back into a bun on her neck that makes her seem so old.

Tina had always thought of her mother as older even than Oma (an impossibility, of course), but Oma was so full of mischief and the love of life, she seemed like a girl of Tina's age.

Maybe when Mama's things came and they settled into the little log house, she might begin to like it here and not fuss at Papa quite so much. Tina hoped so.

Now that Mama had voiced her approval, they doubled their efforts to finish the house. Tina, Wilhelm and Fritz carried buckets of mud from the river bank to Jeff and Papa, who were using the mud to daub the cracks between the uneven logs so that wind and rain could not come through.

"Sometimes the rain washes out the mud," explained Jeff. "Ya just have to get some more and start over again. But it shore helps when the northers blow in!"

Jeff fashioned windows of split logs on heavy leather hinges. "We will get metal ones from St. Louis someday," Papa said. The door of the house was three inches thick and made with flat wood cut by hand. The handle and hinges were a special prize Papa had been able to buy from *Herr* Ernst. He was very proud of their door.

"Next year, after the harvest, we will build another section just like this one, with a dog trot between the two," Papa promised.

Fritz immediately laughed and clapped his hands. "We will get a dog, *ja*, Papa?"

"No, little Fritz," Papa said, smiling. "A dog trot is the name for a sort of porch between the two parts of the log house. We cannot feed a dog, yet, bless us; we cannot even feed ourselves too *gut*."

Frau Ernst lent Mama an old bed and two chairs and a small table from the hotel until their things should arrive. Mama was excited to be getting into her own home finally. Tina was happy to see her mother enthusiastic about something for a change. She went to the hillside and picked a large bunch of the wild flowers she loved so much. Mama had had no time to enjoy them; she would like something so beautiful and colorful in her new home.

Tina carefully put the flowers in an empty bottle she had gotten from *Frau* Ernst and placed them on the rough, un-polished table in the middle of the room. Papa had gone into town to get Mama and make the move into the house official.

Here they were! She could hear the wheels of the little wagon Papa had bought rumbling on the rough road and the bells on Schatzie's bridle tinkling gaily. This was an important moment in their lives, Tina knew. A whole new start for the von Scholl family. Tina heard the boys chattering merrily. Mama and Papa were not saying anything. Both were probably feeling as excited and happy as she was.

Mama walked into the room, her presence filling it. Behind her, Papa's white face looked strained and sad. Tina looked at her mother. She could not believe she was seeing the same woman who had smiled and sung with them yesterday. Her cheeks were pale and sunken in, and her eyes looked bleak. Her lips were compressed tighter than Tina had ever seen them.

What was wrong?

Did Mama, then, hate the house that much? Tina instinctively reached out her hand to her mother.

Mama ignored her and, with heavy steps, marched over to the table where Tina's little bouquet sat. With one movement of her arm she swept the bottle of flowers off the table, crashing to the dirt floor.

"Mama!" Tina cried, her throat constricting and tears very close to the surface. "What is it, Mama?"

Her mother sat down heavily on the rough-hewn straight chair. She took a long, indrawn breath and then spoke in a desolate voice which Tina hardly recognized.

"FIRE! My lovely things, my life, all gone. All burned up in that terrible warehouse in Galveston! *Mein Gott*! All gone! How can I survive in this place without something of beauty to remind me of what I have left behind and what I will never see again?"

With a long, heaving sigh, Mama put her head down on the table. Christina watched her mother weep bitterly for her lost treasures.

M^{AY 15, 1847}

Dear Oma,

. . . and so, dear Oma, that is how it is now. Mama is woe-fully grievous over the loss of all her worldly possessions. As she wept that day, my heart cried out to her. My first thought was to throw my arms about her and say, "Mama, please, don't cry. I will give you my Oma's clock. This will be one thing you will have to remind you of our homeland."

Now is where I blush in shame, Oma. I could not do it. I feel that I must be the most selfish girl in the whole country of America, but I could not bring myself to give away your last gift to me.

I hope that you can understand my feelings. I love Mama dearly, but the clock is the only thing I have ever had of my very own; and you, dear Oma, gave it to me.

How could I ever give it away? Even to Mama? As it was, we all stood around, feeling helpless, while Mama cried her sadness and homesickness out. Papa tried to comfort her, but she would have none of it.

After a while, little Fritz tugged at her skirts and said, "Mama, I'm hungry." That seemed to bring her back to life, and she quickly got up, wiped her face with a towel that hung by the wash basin and went to see what food was in the house.

Without a word Mama prepared dinner, cooking out-of-doors and thinking, I'm sure, about the lovely stove and all her kitchen utensils and dishes which had been destroyed in that fire in Galveston.

I tried to help by setting the table with the dishes Frau Ernst *had lent us and shooing the boys out of the cabin to wait for Mama to announce that supper was ready.*

Papa lit his pipe and quietly sat in front of the little log building, looking off into the distant hills around Industry.

I wondered what his thoughts were, Oma. Nothing had gone the way he planned when he told us of America and the wunderbar *free life we would have in Texas. He must have felt as guilty about bringing Mama here to all this hardship and unhappiness as I do about not being able to give her my clock.*

As we gathered about the table, eating cornbread and boiled beef that was almost as stringy and dry as that we had on the boat, no one had a word to say. I thought my heart was going to break for all of us.

What would we do now, with no furniture, no belongings except the very few that had made it here with us on the trip from Galveston?

Just as we all felt about as dismal as could be possible, Frau Ernst *popped her head inside the open doorway. She is a fine lady,* Frau Ernst, *and has been much help to Mama, both with lending things for our comfort and because she is another woman for Mama to talk to.* Frau Ernst *can understand how it is for us; she and* Herr Ernst *were the first to come to Industry, founding the town after he got his league of land from Mexico, which owned Texas then. They had a very hard life for many years.*

She told us one day about their early life here. "Ah, Emilie," she said to Mama, *"you cannot imagine what it was like back in '31. Our first house was a six-sided mud hut covered with moss and with a sod roof. We had to hold umbrellas over our heads to keep off the rain, ja. We were always repairing that house from the rain and from the cows."*

"Cows?" Mama looked puzzled.

"Ja, cows. They came and ate the moss off the sides of the house. Oh, it was cold in winter! Friedrich tried to build a chimney and fireplace out of logs and clay, but then we never lit it for fear the whole house would go up in flames.

"We had not even the barest necessities of life. No shoes in

winter—later we learned from the Indians how to make mocca-sins or we would trade for them. We had no new clothes, no spinning wheels, and it was twenty-eight miles to San Felipe to go for dress goods. Anyway, there was no money, and calico was fifty cents a yard; do you imagine such a thing?"

The boys and I listened to Frau Ernst and thought how lucky we were, after all. We have a log house and some farm equipment that Papa traded for. We, at least for now, have shoes to wear, although we go with the feet bare every day except Sunday, to save shoe leather.

Talking to Frau Ernst was always good for Mama, so I was very glad to see her in our doorway that sad, first day in our new home.

"Ah, I bother you as you eat, ja? I come back later."

She started to leave, but Mama, the first words she had spoken for a long while, said, "No, no, Louise, stay. Come, eat with us, there is plenty."

Frau Ernst smiled, but declined politely. She told us that she and Herr Ernst were going to give a big party for the von Scholl family at their hotel in Industry. In the big dance hall, it will be held, she said. Next Saturday night, Oma. Isn't that grand?

Mama's eyes lit up with a happy look I have not seen in them since we left Germany. I remembered the parties and dances that she and Papa used to attend at the University. And how beautiful Mama always looked.

Do you remember the emerald green swishy material she had made into a gown? The sleeves were so full and puffy after she stuffed them with paper, she had to go through the door sideways. I thought it the most beautiful gown I had ever seen.

Nowadays Mama wears a black cotton skirt with a loose-fitting jacket over it, an apron tied in back and a cotton sunbonnet. Oma, she does not look anything like the pretty Mama I knew in Germany. But, someday, when things get easier, as they have for Frau Ernst, maybe Mama will be her old self again. And Papa will be happier, too.

I pray for this every night, Oma. And that is why I feel so wicked because I could not give to Mama the only thing of beauty that is left to the von Scholl family now: my clock. I hope you understand and forgive my transgression towards Mama. Please tell me that you do.

I will tell you of the ball—or party—which the Ernsts are giving later. For now,

Your loving Granddaughter,
Christina Eudora von Scholl

. . . Mama's joy about the party did not last long. Her face suddenly clouded over, and she shook her head.

"*Nein*, Louise, we cannot let you do this. Such a lot of work and cost to you."

Frau Ernst would hear of no objections. Mama, her face red with shame, finally admitted, "*Ach*, Louise, we have no proper clothing to wear to such a fine party. All my best dresses and hats were lost in the muddy Brazos River. I have nothing but what is on my back."

"Do not think for a moment on this, Emilie," *Frau* Ernst told Mama. "We are about the same size and I have many dresses which I scarcely wear. Some, old-fashioned now, came with me from Germany sixteen years ago. Come, we will go to my house and look at these dresses.

"There will be something that can be fixed for you to wear and also one that can be remade for our little Christina. She will be the belle of the ball."

Louise Ernst's kind eyes smiled at Tina, who had been holding her breath in fear that Mama would refuse to go to the party.

The next few days flew by in a whirl of activity. Mama's thimble flashed in the sunlight as her fingers guided the needle and thread, in and out, in and out of the dresses *Frau* Ernst had given them. She followed pictures from a magazine to create stylish gowns from old-fashioned ones.

Tina's job was to keep the boys busy and to do the necessary chores and cooking so that Mama's quicker skill in sewing could be used to best advantage as long as daylight held.

Tina watered the vegetable garden, carrying water in buckets-full from the river. She hoped that someday they would have their own well and cistern; it was a half-mile to the river. She fixed supper, cooking whatever Papa and the boys brought in to the house. Sometimes it was a haunch of venison for which they had bartered with some of the nomad Lipan Indians, or jackrabbit which a hunter shared, or sometimes ham or bacon given by a neighbor.

Papa and the boys helped the men with the heavier jobs and did what they could to pay for the food. As soon as Papa's crops came in, they would have something more worthwhile to trade for the provisions they needed. They were guarding carefully the little money they had left.

In the meantime Mama sewed and sewed. By Friday afternoon she called Tina to her.

"Tina, come, you must try on this dress. It is ready for the final hemming and you have grown so tall, I do not know where to put the fold for the hem."

Tina held her breath. She hadn't allowed herself to look at the dress Mama was working on for her. She was almost sixteen, and she was afraid that Mama would make the dress for a girl of twelve or less. Mama had trouble realizing that she was nearly a woman already.

But, for once, Tina was not disappointed. The dress dazzled her eyes when Mama held it up for her to slip over her head.

The fabric, smooth and crisp cambric, was yellow, the shade of newly churned sweet butter, and embroidered with tiny flowers of rose, violet, blue and heliotrope. As Tina smoothed the bodice, with its V-shaped waistline in front, her mother buttoned up the back with many tiny mother-of-pearl buttons. The sleeves were stylishly full from shoulder to elbow, tight fitting to the wrist.

The best part, the skirt, made Tina gasp in enchantment when she saw it. The crisp cambric gathered tightly into the tiny waist and fell in three separate tiers to the floor, each tier fuller than the last.

Tina felt like a princess. *Frau* Ernst had more than kept her promise. Besides the loveliest dress Tina had ever seen, there were four batiste petticoats and a pair of white stockings. Tina could not contain herself, but whirled and curtsied around the room, holding the skirt high above the dirt floor.

"*Ach*, Christina, come, settle down," Mama said, impatient to finish. "I must see how long to make the last ruffle of the skirt. You must put on your shoes, *ja*?

Tina ran to the wooden chest where the family kept their few possessions and carefully extracted the only shoes she owned. Not party shoes. How she longed for some dainty silk slippers, with laces criss-crossed up the ankle! Her skirts would fly when she danced . . . but with these old high leather clodhoppers . . .

"Mama, *ach*, they are too tight, these shoes. I can hardly put my feet in them."

Tina winced as she tied the leather thong laces of the ankle-high shoes.

"It is the foot-bare going, that has done it," Mama said. "There is nothing to be done about it, Tina; your feet have stretched. We have no way to get new shoes and *Frau* Ernst has a very tiny foot. I noticed when we looked at her clothes that day. Well, for the party, it is pinched toes for little Tina, *ja*?"

"I guess so, Mama, but it will be very hard to smile, with these shoes torturing my poor feet. I guess it will be worth it. The dress is so pretty, I will just remember the dress and try to forget the feet, *ja*, Mama?"

"That is true, my Tina; we must always try to count our blessings. Sometimes, it is very hard. I know this."

Mama, immersed in her beloved sewing and thinking of feminine things—gowns and balls—for a change, became closer to being the understanding woman that Tina longed for in her mother.

Tina smiled at Mama, who sat on the floor, pins held tightly between her lips, measuring the hem. As Tina

turned slowly, she daydreamed of the party and wondered how many people would be there and what they
would be wearing and what *Frau* Ernst would serve for
supper.

Oh, it was delightful to have something happy to look
forward to, after the months of hardship and worry.

Even the boys and Papa seemed to be glad about the
party, except for the dressing-up part. Mama had saved
back one little suit for each of the boys, for special occa-
sions. They, too, must try everything on, to see if it still
fit—which it almost didn't in Fritz's case; he had grown so
much all at once! They must try on their shoes, too, after
what had happened to Tina.

Ja, Mama grumbled, they were tight, also. She wished
sometimes she could stop all this growing; it made things
that much harder.

But, of course, she wouldn't have done that, if she
could, thought Tina. We must grow up, and Mama knows
this.

The rest of the week dragged by for Tina. She could not
wait to slip the lovely yellow gown over her head again
and feel like a young lady, the "belle of the ball," *Frau*
Ernst had predicted. Perhaps there would be a boy there,
someone who would dance with her and tell her she was
pretty. And, maybe, have a bit of supper with her, just like
at the the balls in the homeland.

Saturday finally came. The regular chores must be done,
the little house scrubbed, the dirt floor swept. Clothes
must be washed in the river, cooking tended to, the garden vegetables watered and ripe ones picked.

But, then it was time.

Tina and the boys had gone to the river after their work
was done and, stripping down to their underdrawers,
jumped into the cool water and played for a while. Tina
had pinned her long hair up on top of her head so it
wouldn't get wet.

Mama had promised, in the good humor that had lasted

all week, to let Tina wear her hair *up* tonight! She had not expected that special grown-up privilege until her sixteenth birthday on August nineteenth. Her heart was near bursting with excitement.

Using some of Mama's strong, homemade lye soap, Tina bathed in the river, seeing to it that Fritz and Wilhelm washed their necks and behind their ears.

"Mama will check and you will not go to the party if you are not spic and span," she warned.

For once, they complied without grumbling. They had heard of the feasts that *Frau* Ernst was famous for, and nothing would keep them away, not even their hatred of soap.

When they returned to the little house, Papa stood in the doorway, smoking his long, curved pipe, which he took out only on Christmas and holidays. He, too, must be looking forward to this night. His suit, brought from Germany and much too heavy for the Texas climate, was of black wool broadcloth, the long coat hanging below his knees. The breeches were tight-fitting and of the same black material. With his white muslin shirt he wore a black and azure blue striped cravat. Tina thought she had never seen her father look so handsome.

"Oh, Papa, you are so distinguished with your black Sunday suit and your moustache all waxed. I must hurry and get ready, too. The boys and I go now to dress. Where is Mama?"

"*Frau* Ernst sent a driver to pick up your Mama so that they could get things ready for the party. She has already dressed and gone. So lovely, she looked, *Liebchen*. Like the young girl I married." Papa wore a proud look on his face.

"She asked if you can put up your hair yourself? If not, come like that, and she will do it when you get there. We must hurry now. Go, boys, put on your suits and comb the hair nice. Make your mama proud of you, *ja*?"

Tina hurried into the house. Her stockings, petticoats and the lovely dress were laid across Mama's bed. She quickly got into them and then, horrified, wondered how she would button up the back. She was too shy to ask Papa or Wilhelm.

Oh, she wished Mama were here!

Reaching as far behind her as she could, she managed a few of the buttons herself, feeling for the loops as she inched up the back of the dress. She would put her lace shawl—Mama had salvaged that, somehow, from the belongings that had been left to the river—around her shoulders. When she arrived at the Ernsts' hotel, she would ask Mama to finish buttoning her dress.

Ach, she felt beautiful. Even if her feet were going to give her such paining tonight!

Her hair was still pinned loosely atop her head. The sides along her face were tied in rag curlers her mother had fashioned by tearing strips of old fabric and rolling her hair around the material and then tying it in bows to hold the curls.

Tina decided to try to handle this problem herself. She would die of humiliation to appear at *Frau* Ernst's hotel with her hair looking like this and with the white rags still adorning the sides of her cheeks.

Carefully she brushed her long, straight brown hair, highlighted with golden streaks from the Texas sunshine. She braided the back into one long, fat plait, which she wound around her head and fastened with Mama's wire hair pins.

She gently removed the rag curlers. The small sections of hair that they had held in place all day fell into ringlets alongside her face. She put more pins into the heavy braid. Then she took Mama's silver hand-mirror and, holding her breath, looked into it.

"Christina, you look *beautiful!*" Fritz and Wilhelm stood, uncomfortably stiff in their best clothes, shiny-clean and combed with Papa's help, their blue eyes wide with admiration for their sister. It was as if they were seeing her for the first time.

"Do you really think so, boys?" Tina suddenly wanted to be sure that they meant what they said, and weren't teasing her as they so often did.

But Mama's mirror told her that she did indeed look lovely. She would not have known it was the same Tina who this morning was scouring down the kitchen table and chairs till they were bleached white.

She felt like a princess!

"Papa, Papa, come see our Tina!" Fritz cried. "Come see how grown-up she is. She looks like a lady, *ja*?"

Tina flushed with pleasure as her father came from outside into the small cabin to see his daughter in her first ball gown.

M^{AY 30, 1847}

Dearest Oma,

As I promised, I will tell you of the party that the Ernst family gave for us.

Papa, Wilhelm, Fritz and I arrived in the little cart with Schatzie pulling us. Mama had gone on ahead to help Frau Ernst.

Oma, you cannot imagine our surprise as we came into view of the hotel of Herr Ernst! Everywhere were carts and wagons and horses tied to posts. Never have I seen such a gathering here in Texas.

At first we were frightened that something terrible had happened to bring so many people into town. Indians, maybe? When we arrived at the hotel, we discovered that they were all guests of Herr and Frau Ernst—in honor of us, Oma, the von Scholls!

Not only had they traveled for miles, many of them from as far away as Cat Spring and Cummins Creek, but also they had, every one, brought something of their own meager store of goods to share with us. Frau Ernst had sent the message that our belongings had been wiped out in the fire in Galveston and all had, so generously, tried to make up for our loss.

There were pots and pans, dishes, bedding and even a small bed which Fritz can use. The lady with the bed, Frau Wittner, told us that she had lost her little boy to the virulent fever during the winter.

"I will not need the little bed now," she said with a catch in her voice. "Better you should have the use of it, nein?"

Some people brought stores of food, grain and seed. Afterward Papa said that the seed was probably the biggest sacrifice of all for those good people to have made for us.

"Seed corn is hard enough to come by, but rye and wheat seed is almost impossible to get." This was a treasured gift to remember always, Papa said.

Meantime, Mama was exclaiming over some calico for dresses and shirts. And there was a small wagon for the boys. Now they could haul water from the river without carrying it by the bucketful.

For me, there were books. I was so excited by the thought of all the reading I could do, Oma, that for a moment I forgot all about the party.

Just then the fiddlers struck up the music, and everyone moved on into the ballroom to enjoy the evening.

Because of all the excitement over the gifts, I had had no time to notice Mama; but, as she buttoned up the back of my dress, I could see her in Frau Ernst's long mirror.

Oma, I have never seen Mama look so beautiful! Her cheeks were still flushed a pretty pink from the excitement of the gifts and meeting all the neighbors for miles around. She had a tiny little smile on her lips and in her eyes which made her look soft and young again.

The dress Frau Ernst had given Mama was a thing of beauty. The color, Mama said, was violet de Parme, and the fabric, moire. It was of the new fashion, with very tight sleeves and even tighter waistline above a full, gathered skirt. (Mama's waist is smaller than mine, I am ashamed to say, Oma, although one would never guess it in those loose jackets she always wears at home.)

The most beautiful part of the dress was the fine, ivory lace collar which attached to the low V-neckline and was so wide it hung almost to Mama's elbows. Mama looked so feminine and pretty, Oma, in Frau Ernst's little bonnet of shirred and corded silk, in the same shade of lilac, with the ivory silk-lace veil hang-

ing over her dark hair in back, soft curls peeking out next to her cheeks and the silk scarf bow under her chin.

Papa was about to burst with pride for his "two women," he said. Ja, Oma, your little Christina looked very grown-up and felt as beautiful as Mama looked.

After she had buttoned my dress, Mama took some delicate silk flowers of the same colors as the embroidery in the yellow cambric and pinned them in my braid.

"Frau Ernst found these in her trunk," Mama explained. "'For little Christina,' she said."

Yes, Oma, it was a special night for the von Scholl family. The music was lively, and the dancers kept up the rhythm until I thought the floor would surely cave in.

I may not have been the "belle of the ball," as Frau Ernst predicted, but I did have the most magnificent evening of my life. There were so many young people of my age there; I had not seen any of them before. I guess they, like we, have been too busy working just to keep alive, to have time for visiting with their neighbors.

Several of the young men asked me to dance with them. The fiddlers played all the old German tunes; remember "The Pitcher with the Green Wreath?" "Im Krug zum gruenen Kranze?" Was that not one of your favorites? They played that one several times during the evening, along with squares and polkas for dancing.

My pinched toes in my too-small shoes may have been crying, Oma, but I did not hear them, such fun I was having!

Our Jeff came to the party, too. He walked into town from our house, rather than go in the wagon with us. For some reason he became very shy when he put on his Sunday trousers and long-sleeved cotton shirt with a loose tie around his collar.

I thought he would not even nod or speak to me. When I looked at him, he turned away and got very pink in the neck. I walked over to him, very bold for a young woman, and said, in English, "Good evening, Jeff."

He turned to me and said, in very halting German, "Ach, Miss Christina, you look beautiful."

Oma, you are the only person in the whole world to whom I tell this. I am bursting to tell you how I felt at that moment. Jeff has become almost a part of our family, sleeping in the little lean-to behind our house, and sharing our meals and work; but, I must admit, I do not feel like his little sister! I have very strange feelings when I am with this Amerikaner. *That night, at the party, my insides were all fluttery and kind of sick feeling. I tried to say something, but nothing would come out of my mouth.*

Have you ever experienced such peculiar sensations, Oma?

Just as I thought that Jeff and I could talk to one another, Wilhelm and Fritz came bounding up to us and pulled Jeff away to the table to partake of the bounteous feast they could resist no longer.

After they scurried away, Jeff their prisoner, I had such a hollow feeling in my stomach, Oma. I could not have been that hungry. Was it something else I felt?

Ach, I couldn't decide what was my trouble, so I walked to the table and joined Mama and Papa for the wonderful dinner.

I would think about Jeff and the strange actions inside myself later, after the party.

The boys were not disappointed in the feasting. All the guests had brought, not only gifts for our family, but food which the women had spent much time and labor preparing. Believe me, Oma, we all went home from the party happy and thanking the good Lord for such friends and neighbors as we have in this beautiful free land of Texas, America . . . .

. . . It had taken a week or more for the family to come back to earth after the party. Tina would catch Mama standing at the table, her kitchen knife in hand, staring out the small window, daydreaming, a slight smile on her lips. Tina knew that Mama was remembering the evening when for a little while, she had felt a young woman again, and had pretended that their life in America was always as good as that special night had been.

Their little log house looked more like a home once all the gifts were in place. One woman, *Frau* Hoffmann, had

brought Mama a picture to hang on the rough wall of the room.

"We lived in a one-room cabin for six years, *ja*," she said with a smile. "I remember well how lonely I was for something beautiful from home. This lithograph came with me from Germany and was the only thing I had to remind me of the homeland.

"I am happy here now, an *Amerikaner*, so I hope this old picture will help you, too, in the hard times ahead."

Mama could only smile and nod at the woman, so touched she was. Now the picture, its colors faded with age, hung on the wall behind the chair old *Herr* Schumacher had brought as his contribution.

The daily work went on. Jeff and Papa were busy in the field that they had cultivated with the fancy new plow which Papa had purchased for four dollars. Schatzie could pull the plow while Papa followed behind, walking in the deep furrows which would hold their precious winter's harvest.

Although it was too late to plant corn this year, he planted cotton and some tobacco. *Herr* Ernst grew much tobacco and made cigars to sell in New Braunfels and San Antonio.

Jeff kept busy in the fields all day long. The only time that he and Tina saw each other was at meals, and then the boys kept up such a steady stream of chatter, no one could get a word in, Tina thought crossly.

J UNE 17, 1847

Dear Oma,

It is hard to imagine that it is June already, five months since we arrived in Industry, Texas, America. I am loving this beautiful country more and more each day, although I must admit that I had not expected the climate to be so very warm—no, hot—this early in the summer.

We have been very busy harvesting all the spring vegetables in Mama's garden and preserving them for the winter months to come. Mama was able to buy some jars for the canning and we have worked very hard, putting up jams and jellies from wild plums and grapes and have dried some beans and corn and other legumes for winter cooking.

We eat very well these days. Papa, Jeff and the boys catch fish, sometimes, in the river, and Jeff brings a rabbit or 'possum home to be cooked over the open flame.

Papa has promised to order a stove for Mama from Galveston. It may take many months for it to get here, but Mama has become quite skilled at cooking out-of-doors and says she will probably feel cooped up when she must move inside the house to do her cooking.

The boys and I are enjoying the summer weather. When the chores are done, we go to the river for a cooling swim. Sometimes I steal away by myself with one of my precious books and sit on the bank and read. That is my favorite thing to do, Oma, and I am so grateful for all the books our friends shared with us.

Papa is talking of starting a school here. There was an elementary school several years ago, but Papa has also in mind higher grades, even someday, a university.

He has heard of a town to the northwest of us, Sisterdale it is called, which has been started by some of his university professor friends and others who fled Germany, as we did, when trouble threatened.

He hopes to meet with these men and see if we can get support for a school, maybe books and money. Mama says this is a good idea, for the boys need education. I hope, Oma, that I too may go to Papa's school. I want to learn so many more things than I know today.

A secret, Oma. Papa has told me that when he goes to Sisterdale, I may go with him as a reward, he says, for being such a good help to him and Mama.

Is that not a wonderful thing to look forward to? In the meantime, I am content with my books and the blue Texas sky overhead. You should see me, Oma, I am brown as a wood wren and much taller and stronger than when I left you.

And my feet are much larger, as I told you before the party. I am sure Mama is right when she says my feet get bigger the more I walk in the feet bare, but I love the feel of the hot, dry dust between my toes.

Sometimes a yucca spine or thorn is on the ground and it is extracted with great difficulty and pain, but I still enjoy the free feeling it is to go without the shoes on my feet.

Yucca, by the way, is a cactus-like plant, also called Spanish bayonet, that grows wild everywhere in this part of Texas. It has many waxy white, bell-shaped flowers on all sides of its spiny stem. They bloom this time of year and are very beautiful. One of the young ladies in Industry was married last week and her family picked yucca blossoms for her bridal bouquet.

Sometimes the boys come down to the river banks when I am reading and chase green lizards, a hand-span long, or throw stones at alligators sunning themselves on rocks along the river's edge.

Birds fly about us everywhere. The creamy-colored flycatcher, his long forked tail opening and closing like Mama's scissors, swoops overhead. Cardinals, vivid scarlet as their name, bluebirds and blue jays—all come to drink from the little pan I have put on a rock for them. Sometimes they timidly step into the shallow water and then, such a splashing, as they take a bath, like us, to cool off.

My favorites are the tiny hummingbirds, with iridescent green backs and ruby-red cravats on their white chests. They whizz by my head, wings whirring, as they dart from flower to flower, competing with honeybees for the sweet nectar.

And so, dear Oma, things are quiet and serene for the von Scholls. The hard work is still with us, of course, and will be for many years, I am afraid.

Papa is always quoting our famous countryman, Goethe, "It is not doing the thing we like to do, but liking the thing we have to do that makes life blessed."

I guess that must be so, Oma, because I find myself enjoying even the hardest chores, just because we are all here, alive and well, building toward a future in this beautiful, free land . . .

Tina could sense a change within herself, a feeling of movement toward some goal, although the goal eluded her. Her inner feelings bothered her, and she longed to discuss them with Mama. But Mama had gone back into her shell, bitter from comparing what she had left behind with what little she had now, or would ever have, no matter how long or hard they worked.

The party, recalling to her mind so clearly all the things she had sacrificed to come to this new country, actually had made things worse. After the bloom of the evening's happiness had worn off, she became more bitterly German than ever, turning away all suggestions of learning to speak English or to become the least bit *"Amerikaner."*

It saddened Tina to watch her father try to cheer his wife in the long summer evenings, to no avail. Even the boisterous antics of Fritz and Wilhelm did not stir up a smile on her pinched and angry face. She especially seemed to turn away from her daughter, and this puzzled and hurt Tina, who doubled her efforts to please her mother.

And then there was the Night of the Panther.

Rumors that a panther was in the vicinity of the von Scholl's property came to them through Jeff.

"Two boys from down Mill Creek a-ways spotted this panther. Huge he was, light brownish-red in color and with the hoarse *YE-OOW-W* of some tremendous cat."

Jeff did an imitation of the panther's cry. The boys looked impressed.

"They tracked him to the river," Jeff continued, aware that all eyes were on him, "and spotted him in a tree down there, but since they had nothing but a lightweight rifle with 'em and only one shot left, they didn't chance shootin' at him."

Jeff looked worried as he told his listeners that panthers had been known to raid farmyards and to come close to houses in search of food. They killed hogs, chickens and deer and even, Jeff said, had been known to attack horses.

Papa joined Jeff's concern. "I must take your advice, Jeff, and get another gun. All I have is the flintlock I bought when we first arrived in Industry. If I tried to kill a panther with that, I should have to hit him square in the head with the first try, too long it takes to reload and shoot again. He could have me killed and eaten by the time I could send the second shot, *ja?*"

Jeff nodded, grinning at Papa's little jest. "In the meantime," Papa spoke now with a serious face, "I want you children, and you, Emilie, to be especially careful when you go out. Look around and be sure that there is nothing in the trees; they like to lie in wait and then pounce on their victims.

"Also, come, now; we have a lesson in marksmanship, everyone. Time for each to know how to shoot the gun in case I am not here when need arises, *ja?*"

"Are you crazy, Max?" Mama was horrified. "I do not intend to touch that awful weapon, and Tina will not do so either. Also, Fritz is far too young to handle such a gun.

"However, if you so insist, you may show Wilhelm how to shoot; it is probably time he learn to hunt small game and bring provisions home for the table."

Mama was adamant concerning her revulsion toward firearms, and no matter how Papa pleaded, she would not touch the flintlock, or allow Fritz to do so. Fritz cried in disappointment, and finally Mama agreed that he be allowed to watch Papa's demonstration.

"But no shooting, Fritz!" Mama's voice was stern. As for Tina, she was as determined to learn to shoot the gun as Mama was against it. For once, Tina won the battle. Papa argued that it was dangerous not to have one of the women of the household know how to shoot. Who knows when a renegade Indian or outlaw might come to the house when the menfolk were out in the fields?

Mama said no more, but stormed into the house to show her disapproval.

"*Ja*," Papa said as he gathered up the gun, powder, thirty-six caliber lead balls, and powderhorn, "I have been remiss in not teaching all to shoot sooner. Come, we go to the river to practice."

For the next two hours Tina, Wilhelm and Fritz listened to every word Papa told them about the loading and shooting of the flintlock. Jeff lounged on the riverbank, chewing on wild dillweed and grinning at their clumsiness in handling the weapon. Papa had brought some old, cracked bottles and now he set them up on logs between their little group and the river.

"Now," Papa said when he had decided that Tina and Wilhelm knew how to load the gun well enough for the next lesson. "See the target," he said to Wilhelm; "you must load and aim, then shoot that bottle, *ja*?"

As seriously as if his life depended on it, Wilhelm faithfully followed his father's instructions. It took him seven minutes, by Papa's watch, to load the gun.

"*Ach*, Wilhelm," Papa exclaimed, "by now you are dead from the panther, is it not so, Jeff?" At Jeff's nod he continued, "You must practice and practice loading this gun until you can do it quickly, two minutes or less.

"Never mind," he said, seeing Wilhelm's crestfallen face. "Let us see what kind of a shot you are. Try to hit the bottle, *ja*?"

Time after time Wilhelm methodically loaded the flint-lock, took aim and fired at the bottle. It was still cracked, but otherwise unharmed. Wilhelm turned his face away from Papa and the others. His embarrassment and frustration were so great that he could not have tried one more time, no matter if the panther had been sitting there waiting for him to shoot. With disgust he handed the gun to his sister and threw himself down on the ground, head on his knees.

"Do not be discouraged, Wilhelm," Papa spoke kindly to his eldest son. "Papa is not the good marksman that is Jeff. I, too, must practice at loading the gun and shooting.

Perhaps that is why I have never taken you out before now, to learn for yourself. Embarrassed, I was, at how clumsy I am.

"But this life is new to all of us, my son. Come, let us help Tina now." At Papa's words, Wilhelm's face cleared of its unhappiness as he turned to watch his sister.

Tina hated to try to load and shoot the gun. She wished Jeff would go away. She would die of humiliation if she could not do it; what would he say? Would he tease her? Would he laugh?

Gritting her teeth in determination, Tina went through each step of the loading process as she remembered her father's instructions. No one said a word, which added to her discomfiture. Finally, she was ready to try hitting the target. The bottle seemed to have shrunk, so small it looked as she sighted the gun.

"*Ach*, papa, I did not realize how heavy this gun is,"

Tina said, wishing that she had listened to Mama and stayed at home.

The gun weighed heavily on her arms as she held it up to take aim. She found herself shaking, with the weight of the gun and the effort to aim at the bottle. But the thought of Jeff, quietly watching through half-closed lids, maybe mocking her, gave her the added strength to hold the gun very, very still as she concentrated on the bottle that now seemed so far away.

Wh—u—mpf!

The gun went off and the bottle shattered, almost, it seemed to Tina, at the exact same moment. She wondered if someone had broken the bottle, just to tease her.

With a questioning look in her eyes, she turned to her father, and beyond him, to Jeff and the boys. All four males wore the same expression on their faces. *Astonishment*!

Fritz was the first to find his voice. "Tina, you did it, you did it! Look, Papa, Tina hit the bottle! Tina is the marksman, *ja*, Papa?"

"*Ja*, indeed, Fritz," Papa said with a broad smile for Tina. "This is very good, my daughter; I am proud of you. Now you must try one more time, to be sure it was not accident."

Jeff had a big grin on his face, but Tina's heart went out to poor Wilhelm. A girl had beaten him at a man's job, and the disgrace mortified him. He would not look at Tina but pretended to be very busy buttoning and unbuttoning his jacket.

Papa set up a second bottle. Tina spent the next few minutes loading the gun and then, when she was ready, stepped back to the spot Papa had designated and took careful aim.

As she steadied her arm against the weight of the gun, she knew, without a doubt, that she could hit the bottle again. It was easy, just aim and pull the trigger. There was nothing to this shooting business.

At that moment, Tina thought of Wilhelm, so unhappy over his failure and her success. As she squeezed the trigger, Tina felt herself pull slightly to the right of target. This time there was only the noise of the gun to prove that she had pulled the trigger. The green bottle still glistened in the sun on its log platform.

She had missed.

There was no shouting. No one said anything. It must have been an accident that first time, *ja*? Tina was sure Papa, her brothers and, worst of all, Jeff were convinced of it at this moment.

She saw a small smile creep onto Wilhelm's face.

"Come, everyone, it gets late," Papa broke into the silence. "We practice some more another day soon until we are good shots, *ja*?"

Papa had no way of knowing that Tina and her brothers would have to use what little knowledge they had of firearms and of the flintlock so soon.

57

T HREE days had gone by since the practice session with the rifle. Mama had

THREE days had gone by
since the practice session
with the rifle. Mama had

been stubbornly silent about the affair, so that Tina had had no opportunity to tell of her success with shooting the gun.

Papa and Jeff had gone to town with Schatzie's cart full of tobacco for market. A wholesaler from Houston was said to be coming through that day or the next, and they wanted to sell their first small crop before a rain or a norther could ruin it.

"We may not be back until late tomorrow, Emilie," Papa said as they hitched the wagon to Schatzie. "I hope to get a good price for the tobacco. We need the money for winter supplies.

"Tina, Wilhelm, Fritz, you must help Mama. Do whatever you can to make her life easier. Do you hear your papa?"

"*Ja*, Papa," chorused the boys as Tina nodded her head and smiled a shy goodbye to Jeff.

The day passed swiftly, with added chores for all. After supper Mama said she was going to bed early.

"*Ach*, I feel tired tonight, Tina. You do the go-to-bed chores, *ja*, and put the boys down for the night."

Tina glanced sharply at her mother, thinking that never before had Mama done so. Perhaps she missed Papa's presence in the house.

"*Ja*, Mama. I will take care of everything," Tina replied gently. She worried about Mama and her health.

The boys quietly played games in the corner where the lantern still glowed while Tina completed the night-time chores.

"Come, Fritz, Wilhelm, we must go to bed now. I am afraid the light and our voices will disturb Mama and awaken her," Tina whispered as she glanced over at her mother's slumbering form.

Tina snuffed out the remaining candle that burned on the table and extinguished the flame in the lantern. Slowly she began to undress. Somehow she felt tired tonight, too.

As she sat on the edge of her bed, in her camisole and petticoat, brushing her long thick hair, she thought she heard a noise.

"Hush, boys, to sleep now."

"Tina, that was not us. We are very still," Wilhelm's voice from across the room complained. "I too hear a noise. It sounds as though it comes from the chicken pen, *ja*?"

"I hear it too," Fritz said, not wanting to be left out. Three pairs of ears strained to hear the noise once more.

Yes, Tina nodded, it was from the back of the house. Probably the new chickens Papa had just brought home had been spooked by something. They were restless, nervous creatures.

With a sigh, Tina decided to look out back and see what was ruffling the feathers of the chickens at this time of night.

"I will go check on the noise," Tina said to the boys in a low voice.

"No, Tina, I must go," Wilhelm said. "Did not Papa tell me that I am the man of the house while he is gone?"

"I, too, must go check on the noise, Tina." Fritz scrambled out of his little bed and stood beside Wilhelm, trying very hard to look as tall as his older brother.

Tina smiled. It would be good for them to take some responsibility; they were growing bigger each day.

"Yes, Will, you go settle the hens on their roost," she said. "And, Fritz, if you are very quiet and don't wake Mama with your loud chatter, you may go with Will. Hurry, so that we can all get to sleep."

Tina waited in the dark room as the boys tiptoed toward the door. Quietly they left the cabin and crept around to the back yard.

Tina waited for their return, deliciously snuggling into the familiar hollows of her horsehair mattress.

Suddenly she sat bolt upright.

From the back of the house came an immense cat-noise, "YEEE-OWWW-WW" and the sound of scuffling, scurrying feet.

The boys burst into the cabin, breathless and, for once, speechless. Tina had sprung from her bed and run to the corner of the room where Papa had left the flintlock. She had never heard a sound like the one from the back yard, but she knew what it was, without any doubt.

"The panther!" Will found his voice, but it came out in a croak. "Tina, what shall we do? The panther is in the back yard. He has already killed one of our new chickens! Oh, I wish Papa and Jeff were here!"

"Hush, Will," Tina whispered as she pulled the boys into the safety of the house and closed the thick door after them. "Mama is stirring. You will awaken her with your loudness.

"Now we must think about this. I will take the gun and go out and shoot the panther . . . . "

As she spoke in low, calm tones, Tina gathered up the powderhorn and powder, the box of thirty-six caliber lead balls and the tiny square of fabric Papa had called the "patch."

"Tina, no! You must not try it." Fritz tugged at Tina's white petticoat and tried to keep her from leaving the house. "It is so dark out there, and the beast was right in the back yard when we went around the corner."

"Fritz is right." Will's face was as white as Tina's underclothes as he whispered to his sister. "The panther is huge, Tina, the largest thing I have ever seen. I think we frightened him, because when he heard us coming he bounded into the big live oak tree. You mustn't try to shoot him. *You can't!* You have only fired the gun two times in your life."

"Will, I must," Tina said. "If I don't, he will kill all our precious chickens—and, even worse, he might attack one of us. I must kill him."

Tina spoke with the stubbornness she displayed rarely, but as Oma used to say, "When she does, *watch out!* The sparks will fly for certain."

Now she had no time for arguments, no time for fear. The chickens and indeed the family were in danger, and she alone could do anything about it.

"Stay here," she commanded Fritz and Will. "I will be right back."

With difficulty she hoisted the heavy gun over her shoulder and picked up the ammunition box and powderhorn. She must not load the gun until she was sure the panther was still there. Papa had said, "Never load the gun unless you know that you are about to shoot it."

As she started toward the door, both boys followed close behind her.

"We come with you, Tina. You must not go out there alone." Will's face took on a look of determination to match Tina's. Fritz fearfully bobbed his head in agreement.

Without speaking, Tina nodded. The three silently crept out the door and started on the frightening trip around the house to the backyard.

Although their eyes were accustomed to the darkness, they could see nothing, so jet-black it was. Tina wished with all her heart that it had been a moonlit night. That same heart seemed to have stopped beating as they crept silently along, feeling the familiar rough logs of the house to guide their way.

Around the corner now . . . careful . . . make no noise.

"Can you see him?" Tina asked Will.

"No, it's too dark. Maybe he ran away, *ja*, Tina?" Will's voice, low as it was, sounded hopeful.

YEEEE-OOOWW-WW. . . .

The boys scrambled to clutch their sister, almost making her drop the gun. The three retreated around the corner of the cabin.

"Shhh . . . he's still in the live oak," Tina said, her heart having started such a pounding so loud, she was afraid the panther crouched in the tree could hear it.

"Quick, Will, go get the lantern. I can see nothing here. I must load the gun like Papa taught us and hope the panther waits for me!"

Will's body was a streak of soft sound in the darkness, a darkness to be felt, so thick was its veil over familiar things which now seemed unfamiliar to Tina as she waited.

After what seemed like a lifetime, Will came around to the side of the house with the lighted lantern, its glow preceding him with a feeling of safety. It was good to be able to see somewhat, Tina thought.

Will and Fritz took turns holding the lantern, while Tina searched her brain for every word that Papa had taught them about the flintlock.

"To load," she said, "I must first put some gunpowder down the bore, *ja*?"

The boys nodded their heads like two marionettes. Tina, hands shaking and mouth dry, lifted the powderhorn and sifted some of the black powder into the bore. She took one of the lead balls out of its box and started to drop it down the bore after the powder.

"*Ach*!" She shook her head. "I almost forgot the patch. Quick, hand it to me, Fritz, the little square of cloth there in the box. Now, let me see, Papa said to spit on the patch. *Ach*, I have no spit in me. My mouth is as dry as the powder horn itself.

"Quick, Will, spit! Spit on the cloth. We must hurry." Tina's voice had so much urgency in it, even in its low whisper, that Will took the little square of cloth and, as though spitting were the most important thing he would ever be asked to do, managed to get the patch good and damp. "To keep a space between ball and powder," Papa had said.

"*Gut!* Now the ramrod."

Tina withdrew the brass ramrod from the brackets on the side of the rifle and gingerly pushed the end down into the bore, tamping it a few times.

She hoped that was how she was supposed to do it. It was a little fuzzy now, her remembering. The fear that the big cat would leap across the clearing and attack them before she had the gun ready was now very real.

Afraid to hurry too fast and misfire for any reason, she forced herself to concentrate on the final stages of loading the flintlock.

As her fingers worked clumsily, her father's patient voice sounded in her ears, explaining over and over: "The little pan there on top of the gun, the flash pan, must be opened and filled with gunpowder. See, Tina, the lid, the frizzen, comes up and we place gunpowder so; then, put the frizzen back down and we are ready to cock the gun."

"But, why, Papa, do we need the flash pan loaded if the gun itself is loaded?" Tina remembered asking her father that.

"When the trigger is pulled," he had said, "the flint on the end of the hammer comes down, and the frizzen comes up, causing a spark to ignite the powder in the flash pan.

"That spark goes down to gunpowder in the barrel and explodes, sending the lead ball to its target. Is it not clever, the flintlock?" Papa had been so proud of his explanation of a gun of which he was not too sure himself.

Now Tina was thankful that her father was such a good teacher. Carefully she pried open the frizzen and, again taking the powderhorn from little Fritz who was plainly shaking now, she filled the flash pan with gunpowder and closed the frizzen.

"Now," she said, with a sigh, "we are ready to cock the hammer, so, and then it is only for the panther that we must wait.

"Quickly, Wilhelm, hold the lantern as high as you can. We will creep softly around the corner and, maybe we will see this monster cat, *ja?*" In her excitement and fear, Tina had reverted to speaking German, something she hadn't done, except to Mama, for weeks now.

Will, with Fritz following, moved silently from behind Tina and, on tip-toe, held the lantern high before him.

There he was.

All they could see were two yellow eyes, seeming to stare right at them. No other part of the animal could they discern—only those two malevolent amber eyes.

Heaving the gun up onto her shoulder, Tina took steady aim. Had her success that other time been an accident? What if this time she missed? Would the panther attack the three human beings who threatened him?

She must not miss.

HOLDING her breath, Tina looked down the barrel of the flintlock exactly between those two yellow globes shining in the inky night. With the forefinger of her right hand, she smoothly pulled the trigger. The gun snapped.

Wh—u—mpf!

For a long moment, stillness filled the air. Not even a leaf moved on the big oak tree. Then Tina heard a CRASH and a loud thud.

Beside her the boys gave out a whoop!

"He has fallen from the tree, Tina. He is dead!"

"You have killed the panther, Tina, look, look!" Tina realized that, at the moment of firing, she had closed her eyes so tight that now they hurt as she forced herself to look. With the boys shouting, she opened them to see. . . .

There he lay, still and dead, the panther. His tawny-beige body stretched out to enormous size; strong, sinewy legs that had borne him on many a hunt would move no more. Tina felt a surge of pity for the beautiful animal.

If he had only stayed in the woods and not threatened all that was dear to her. . . .

"*Ach,* what is the noise? Why are you out here? What has happened?"

Mama's shrill voice came rushing around the corner of the house, with Mama fast behind it.

"Look, Mama," Fritz cried proudly, "come see the panther which we have killed. Isn't it huge, Mama, the panther?"

The boys stood holding the lantern over the panther, like wild-game hunters surveying their kill. Will, feet apart and hands on hips, looked brave and fearless as he studied the huge animal, so still beneath his gaze. Fritz danced and pranced around the beast's body, a near-primitive celebration of the hunt.

Tina stood motionless, heart and mind suspended in space, hardly aware of what she had done, a numbness replacing the taut nerves and raw fear of moments before. Slowly she turned to hear what Mama's reaction would be.

"Oh, *mein Gott!*" Mama sounded near fainting. She took one look at the prone body of the big cat and rushed to gather the boys to her. With tears falling, she moaned and sighed, "*Ach,* you could have been killed. Tina, why did you let the boys come out here? It was too dangerous! That panther could have attacked at any moment. I told your papa it was no *gut,* the gun."

Without another word for the stricken girl, Mama led the two boys inside the house.

Gathering the gun and its equipment as best she could in the darkness, Tina trudged into the cabin, dejected and forlorn.

Not a word from Mama about how well she had done. Not a word of worry for her safety . . . only the boys. Always the boys. It wasn't fair.

She put the gun in its corner; she would clean it like Papa had taught them in the morning. Now she would creep into bed and try to sleep.

Mama was crooning a soft song to little Fritz to calm him down. Will had already fallen fast asleep. Tina's eyes remained open in the darkness for most of the night, covers pulled up to her chin to keep the chill she felt from making her teeth chatter. It was nearly dawn when her tear-filled eyes finally closed from sheer exhaustion, and she slept.

Papa and Jeff returned about noon the next day. The

boys ran to meet the cart and act as news-bearers. Tina could hear their chatter and Papa's excited voice. She made no move to go out to join them.

Mama had not mentioned the night's activities again. It was as though if she ignored the panther lying out there under the tree, it would never have been. Even when Papa called excitedly for them to come and see it in the daylight, she refused to go.

Papa called again.

"Emilie, Tina, come to see this gigantic animal. He was a beautiful specimen; I'll give him that."

Tina walked slowly outside and around the house, her desire to see the beast by daylight overcoming her hurt feelings.

As she turned the corner of the cabin and saw Papa and Jeff looking down at the panther's body, she could not believe that the events of the previous night had been real—or that she had indeed killed this tremendous cat.

"Tina, look at this animal," Papa said with exhilaration in his voice. "Jeff has paced it off and, from tip of nose to end of tail, he measures near *nine feet*."

"Yeah," Jeff spoke up, looking impressed for the first time since Tina had known him, "and he weighs two hundred-fifty pounds, if he weighs an ounce. I'd wager a month's pay on it."

"Wilhelm," Papa spoke to his eldest son with pride, "you have done well, last night. I do not know how you did it, but the fact is that the cat lies there, dead, from one thirty-six caliber lead ball right between the eyes."

Tina watched Will's face as it churned with emotions of pride, guilt and disappointment. She said nothing.

"Papa, I must tell you," Will began with hesitancy, hating to lose that look on Papa's face, of satisfaction in his elder son . . . hating to give up the moment of glory that did not belong to him, but was so sweet.

"Yes, my son?" Papa said, listening.

"Papa, it was not I who killed the panther. It was Tina.

"She was so brave and kept Fritz and me brave, too. She

remembered everything you taught us about the flintlock, Papa, and with one shot, killed the beast. *Ja*, Tina it was who killed the panther."

A moment of silence followed, the shock of Will's words sifting into Papa's consciousness. His daughter, Tina, had killed the giant wild panther?

All eyes were upon Tina.

She could not say a word. But somewhere deep inside of her, a tiny voice prayed, "Let Papa be proud of me."

There was soon no doubt of Papa's feelings toward his daughter, the panther-killer. He rushed to her side and gave her a tight bear-hug and even swung her off her feet and around and around. Tina caught a glimpse of the boys, as they stood clapping and laughing, and of Jeff who had the largest grin known to man on his face.

Afterwards for an hour or more, they all sat around the table discussing the previous night's events, with Papa telling them over and over again how proud he was of them, and especially of Tina. She basked in his pride of her, and only the tiniest bit of her was still unhappy about Mama's reaction.

Mama was still silent. She believed the panther would have wandered off by himself had they not disturbed him.

"All of them, *ja*, all, could have been killed, Max," was all she would add to the day's conversation.

Jeff had unharnessed Schatzie from the cart and saddled her, riding into Industry to spread the news that the panther was dead and that a mere slip of a girl, not even sixteen yet, had pulled the trigger, sending the cat to its death in the middle of the night.

Soon neighbors began to arrive to view the carcass of the marauder, and all exclaimed how brave Tina had been. Mama and Tina were busy all day, feeding the visitors and offering them coffee.

It is almost like a holiday, thought Tina happily. She kept quiet and merely smiled at all the accolades heaped on her by the visitors. The only time she said anything was when the men decided to move the carcass of the panther out to an open meadow and leave it there.

"For the buzzards to pick clean," they said.

"No," Tina spoke up with a firm, clear voice. Then more quietly, surprised at her vehemence, she said to her father, "Papa, no, please. Do not leave the cat to the buzzards. Could you not bury it, Papa? It was such a proud, magnificent animal. Please."

No one spoke a word. No one laughed at her girlish foolishness over a dead beast that could have killed her with one swipe of its paw.

Papa looked at the other men. Softly he spoke to his daughter, "All right, Christina, we will bury the animal. He was, after all, king of his world, was he not? And, a king deserves a burial, *ja*."

It took all the men with the boys trying to help to lift the heavy animal onto Schatzie's cart. Then, following the cart on horseback, they set out to find a place in the woods to dig a burial hole for the huge beast.

Tina felt grateful for Papa's gentle understanding of her feelings.

The Night of the Panther was over, but it had been the most exciting adventure of Christina Eudora von Scholl's young life.

I NDUSTRY, Texas
August 2, 1847

Dear Oma,

Forgive me for not writing as often as I promised. The summer has been so busy, I can hardly believe July is over and my sixteenth birthday is fast approaching.

After all the excitement of **Frau** *Ernst's party and the danger of the Night of the Panther, life has settled down to a sort of busy hum-drum.*

We are never idle, there is so much to be done, but the work is dull and tiring. Sometimes, I fear, I yearn to run away to the meadow and throw myself down on the green carpet laughing with flowers and do nothing but lie there and daydream.

Isn't that a wicked thing to wish, Oma, when I know how much work there is for all to share?

The early garden has been harvested, but now come on the later vegetables—carrots and beets—and Mama's herbs—basil, thyme, sorrel and caraway.

Ach, I almost forgot to tell you. We now have a milch *cow and calf. It was a festive day when Papa came home leading the gentle cow—Fritz named her Daisy, in honor of the white and yellow wildflowers with which we make chains and crowns for our hair—and her calf, Nellie.*

Will is our new **Amerikaner** *name for Wilhelm, but Mama must not hear us call him so. He decided on Nellie for the pretty little calf in honor of a girl by that name in Industry.*

We tease Will about his two Nellies, and he blushes and runs away from Fritz and me. In a way, I understand him, though. I would be embarrassed if the brothers, or anyone, teased me about my feelings for Jeff.

Those feelings, Oma, I do not understand. But for now, I bury them deep within me and continue my everyday life.

Oh yes, I was telling about the cow. It is my job, the milking of Daisy, and I rather enjoy it except for the flies that swarm around us as she slip-slops her stream of warm milk into my bucket. Then, when we have enough milk for the family's use, I put her into the pen with Nellie who is happy to have her mama again—and her supper.

Another thing I now do is to churn the butter from Daisy's sweet cream. Mama bought a wooden churn in town and I have become very good at knowing just when to stop at the moment the butter is exactly right. I am very proud of my butter, which we sometimes sell to some of our Amerikaner *neighbors.*

Mama cannot understand why the Texians do not bother to have vegetable gardens or milch *cows for fresh milk and butter. And the rich buttermilk . . . mmm. She says she has never seen the like of the "lazy-ness. How can they live so, on nothing but corn and pork?"*

Papa bartered for some chickens and we have eight hens and a rooster—no, seven hens; the panther killed one of them. Fresh eggs each day, Oma. So good they taste. Now we can do more cooking, with our own eggs and cream and butter.

I must go now, Oma, the light begins to dim, and I will have to hurry to bring Daisy from the field and get the milking done before dark.

I will try to be better at writing. For sure, I will let you know how goes my birthday on August nineteenth.

Sixteen, Oma. Can you imagine?

Your loving,
Christina Eudora von Scholl

. . . Sixteen. The magic year. Tina had dreamed of being sixteen for as long as she could remember. It meant the start of her life as a woman. Many of her friends in Germany would marry soon after their sixteenth birthdays.

Here in America, she supposed it was the same, but she had met no young women of her age with whom she could talk. She often found herself longing to see her friend, Lisette, in Oldenburg.

She had so many wonderings inside of her. She wished she could talk to Mama. . . .

Tina sat on the little wooden stool, her cheek resting against Daisy's warm side. The rhythm of the milk streams against the metal pail beat a steady accompaniment to her thoughts.

The hot summer days followed swiftly, one upon the other, until August nineteenth was finally upon them. Mama had not mentioned Tina's birthday, so it was with misgivings that the day began. Perhaps the family had forgotten. Would she be able to pretend that she did not care?

Tina sometimes felt that she spent most of her life pretending that she did not care: that Mama seemed to favor the boys over her; that she had no time for friends of her own age; that she would never see her grandmother again. How she longed to talk to Oma just now, on her sixteenth birthday, to tell her all the secrets she could share with no one else.

Papa and Mama had set out early in the morning with Schatzie pulling the little cart.

"To see *Frau* Ernst," Mama said.

"To buy supplies for the next few months," Papa said. Whatever their purpose in going, Tina was left with the responsibility of watching over the two younger brothers and of doing her everyday chores, plus what Mama would have done this day. Tina bit her lip, feeling guilty for the rebellious thoughts which came unbidden to her mind.

Of all days, why did they choose this one, her most important birthday, to go off to town and not even invite her to go along?

Glumly, she went about the business of milking, churning, cleaning and cooking. She sent the boys to the river for water, feeling a jab of anger at their laughter as they pulled the wagon with its jugs bouncing.

Even they, her two brothers, had forgotten what day it was. Well, no one would ever know from her that her feelings were hurt. It was, after all, just another day on the calendar, wasn't it?

Feeling sorry for herself, Tina decided to take down her precious clock from the wall and wind and polish it. She found Mama's store of beeswax which she had been hoarding for use on her fine old dining room table and chairs when they would arrive from Galveston. Now, the beeswax was of no use to Mama. There would be no fine furniture in the little log cabin. Only the rough cedar pieces which the Ernst family had lent them and the handmade oak furniture some of the neighbors had given them at the party.

The only thing left to be waxed and lovingly cared for was her clock. Tina wound it each day and often waxed and rubbed it to a burnished gloss which shimmered like the finest silk-satin, giving back the candle's glow in soft reflection.

Tina sat, thinking and polishing, long after the clock's every flat and deeply carved surface had been carefully rubbed with the soft flannel cloth she kept just for this task. Thinking of Oma and how much she missed her; about Texas and how hard their life had been so far; about her future here and what it might hold for her and her only possession, the little cuckoo clock. She thought, too, about Jeff and wondered again why his face kept coming into her mind when she least expected it.

Finally she roused herself from her reverie and carefully replaced the clock on its nail driven into the rough log wall, so out of place here, yet so important to her happiness and somehow, she felt, tied into her future.

Would Oma's clock help her to grow up, truly, and to face whatever fate had in store for her? Straightening it gently with her finger tips, Tina thought she could feel Oma's love in the smooth wood and hear a message only for her in the quiet, rhythmic ticking.

At dusk, as Tina finished setting the table for supper, wondering if Mama and Papa would even be there for the meal she had prepared or would stay at *Herr* and *Frau* Ernst's to sup with them, she heard Schatzie's bridle bells tinkling in the distance and the boys' voices raised in salute to their returning parents.

"Mama, Papa, you are home," Fritz's high voice rose above Will's. "We thought you were lost on the way, so late you are."

Papa's greeting to the boys was jovial and even Mama said something which Tina could not hear but which had a happy ring to the tone of it. Tina thought the parents must have had a lovely time in Industry today. She tried very hard to be happy for them for she knew they deserved it; but the little voice of unhappiness would not be quelled, and she could not put a smile upon her face as the family came trooping into the cabin, Papa first, then Mama, with the boys noisily behind.

As Tina kept at her chores, unable to greet her parents for the lump in her throat, the boys set up a clamor.

"Tina, Tina, come see. See what you have, Tina, for your sixteenth birthday."

They had remembered, after all.

As Tina turned, astounded, Papa came and kissed her gently on the cheek, with a soft, "Happy Birthday, dear Christina."

Mama, a quiet smile playing at the corners of her lips, put her arms around Tina and said, "*Ja*, Daughter, a Happy Birthday to our sixteen-year-old. *Ach*, it seems but yesterday you were a tiny babe in my arms, little Tina. May you always be happy."

Tina's eyes glistened with tears as she returned her mother's brief hug. Never had Mama said such words to her. Never had she given of her love as at this moment. Tina wanted to make it last, to hold this feeling of being loved forever and ever.

As usual, the boys broke the spell with their boisterous yelling. "Come, Tina, come see. You have gifts to open. And another surprise besides."

They pulled and yanked, each at one of Tina's arms, until, laughing, she let them lead her to the table where several bundles lay. With a glance toward her mother, who smiled and nodded her head, Tina shyly started to pull the string from the bundle which was wrapped in brown paper. She could hardly see what she was doing; each boy's head was leaning over the table almost on top of the package. Papa pulled them by the trousers.

"*Ach*, you two, it is Tina's birthday, not yours. Let her have peace and unwrap her gifts for herself."

Reluctantly the brothers backed away, keeping up a steady stream of giggling and whispering. Tina was having trouble with the knots of the store string which must be kept and added to the ball of twine, slowly growing as they saved each bit that came their way. Finally the stubborn knot yielded, and the paper fell open. Tina caught her breath.

New shoes.

"Oh, Mama, Papa. I love you. Shoes! Now I have shoes to wear when we go to town. Thank you, thank you. They are the most beautiful shoes I have ever seen."

Tina could not believe her eyes. The shoes, ankle-high boots really, were of tan canvas-like fabric, with fashionable flat heels and gussets of elastic in the sides for pulling on. Best of all, they had dainty, pointed toes of black leather.

Ach, such shoes!

Tina sat down on the kitchen chair to try them on, but the boys would have none of it.

"Tina, look, more presents to open yet!" Will could not wait for the shoe-trying-on to take place. He pushed the other package, this time a large box, in front of Tina.

"Open, open!"

Tina smiled happily at her brother and untied the string. She pulled the lid off the box slowly, wanting to savor the happiness of this moment, to make it last as long as possible. Finally she dared peek into the box.

"A bonnet!"

Oh, it was too much. Mama and Papa had spent a fortune on her. And she had been feeling so sorry for herself.

Carefully she lifted the hat from its tissue-lined box and, with a sigh of happiness, put it on her head. With a quick look of gratitude to her parents, she ran to her mother's chest of drawers and picked up the silver hand mirror.

It was beautiful . . . exquisite . . . there were no words to describe it, or how she was feeling at this moment. Like . . . like someone who is loved . . . like a young woman ready to meet whatever life has in store for her . . . like. . . .

"It is the new style, Christina," Mama's voice broke into Tina's thoughts, "just brought to Industry by *Frau* Albrecht, who is starting a shop here. The shape of the straw is called a coal scuttle, because that is what it looks like, *ja*? *Frau* Albrecht says the flowers at the sides of your face and the lace veil in back will make you look very feminine. This is true. Here, let me tie the ribbons, so! *Ja*, very pretty you look.

"But come, time to eat the meal now. After supper you can be the peacock again and preen your feathers, *ja*?"

Tina threw her arms around her mother's thin shoulders. "Mama, Mama, you should not have spent so much of our precious money on me. Perhaps you should return the bonnet. I will be so happy with the new shoes. That would have been enough."

"No, Christina," Papa spoke up. He had been sitting at the table watching the proceedings with a proud smile on his face.

"Your Mama and I wanted to make your sixteenth birthday a special event in your life. Fortunately we were able to barter with *Frau* Albrecht, who has no garden or animals yet. She was very happy to trade us for eggs and milk and even some of your famous butter. So you see, you helped pay for the presents yourself."

Tina smiled with gratitude at her father's kind words, but she knew that those things could have been bartered for items more necessary to the family than fancy bonnets and pretty shoes. The knowledge of their sacrifice meant more to her than the gifts themselves.

She replaced the bonnet in its box, carefully folding the deep green ribbons which would tie under her chin and gently touching the fragile pink silk flowers on the inside of the brim of the buff straw "coal scuttle."

She busied about, getting supper on the table, listening to the boys' chatter and watching Mama out of the corner of her eye. Never had Mama shown her so much affection.

Glowing with happiness, she called, "Supper's ready."

SUPPER over, Tina cleaned up the dishes and put them in the small side- board they had fashioned from an old chest that had been part of the Ernsts' party gifts. In it they kept their few pieces of crockery and the one tablecloth they had salvaged, along with the forks and knives, spoons and serving pieces they had gathered together.

Tina knew each time Mama looked at the chest with its meager contents, she mourned for the loss of her fine belongings from Germany. Tonight Tina could think of nothing but how happy she was and how grateful to her family for remembering her special day.

As she bustled about, Tina became aware of the boys' eyes following her every move.

"Are you finished yet, Tina? Hurry, there is yet another surprise for your birthday." Fritz was squirming with excitement, and Will was whispering something to Papa.

"Papa? What is it?" Tina did not believe she could stand another ounce of happiness, another surprise. Her heart was already full to bursting.

"Come, my Tina," said her father, smiling. "Sit beside me. A special letter has come for you, a week ago already. It was for your birthday, so your Mama and I decided to keep it for you until today.

"Here, read. It is from your Oma."

Without a word, her feelings too deep to express, Tina

took the envelope from her father's hand and sat in the rocking chair beside him. Slowly she withdrew the letter and looked at the small, spidery handwriting through her tears.

How could Oma have planned it so well, to get a letter here just in time for her sixteenth birthday?

"Dearest Christina," she read aloud, "*Gott* be with you on this very important day of your life, your sixteenth birthday.

"From today you are a woman grown, and a beautiful one, I know, although we have not seen each other for many months. The seeds for beauty, of face and of spirit, were there always, my Tina, and they have sprouted through the years and grown, and now you blossom like a lovely flower in the summer garden.

"How I miss you and would love to see you today, to share in your happiness. . . ." Tina's voice broke, and she looked up at Papa whose eyes were damp with unshed tears.

"You must keep that happiness in your heart, little granddaughter," Tina continued reading. "Take care of the papa and the brothers, now that you are able. Most of all, take especial care of your mama in the difficult days ahead for her.

"I wish you all the blessings that you deserve. Write to me often, Christina. Do not forget your little Oma."

No one said a word. Tina silently refolded the thin paper and replaced it in the envelope. She would keep it always, this letter, and try to live up to her grandmother's expectations of her.

There would be much to think about tonight, after she crawled into her bed in the corner of the big room.

The boys began a game of cards. Papa reached for his everyday pipe and lit it, settled into the chair nearest the candle and opened a book. Mama let the pins out of her long, dark hair and unbraided it. Taking the silver brush which matched her mirror, she brushed and brushed her one claim to beauty, thick, chestnut tresses that fell to her hips.

Tina thought how quiet and peaceful it was, here in the little log house in Texas. But she could not settle down. She wanted to sing and dance and twirl in circles; her happiness was so great.

"I am going out for a little walk, Mama. Is it all right? I am too excited; it will calm me to walk in the night air," Tina asked her mother who nodded, hairpins between her lips.

Outside the summer evening was hot, no air moving. The August moon was full and shed a silvery blanket over everything, making it difficult to recognize even ordinary landmarks. Tina walked slowly, scuffing the night-cool dust with her bare feet, remembering that in the excitement she had forgotten to try on her new shoes.

It had all seemed like a dream—the shoes, the bonnet and the loving letter from Oma. She thought of what her grandmother had said. What had she meant when she said of Mama, " . . . in the difficult days ahead of her?" Would not the days be as hard for them all? Why single out Mama? Perhaps just because Oma still thought of Mama as her little daughter, *ja*? Perhaps.

As she walked through the brightly lit night, she heard a noise ahead of her. Realizing that she had come farther than usual from the safety of the house, without the security of the gun, she felt a ripple of fear.

Could it be Indians? Or an animal?

She stood stock-still, hardly breathing.

"Tina? What are you doing out h'yer so far from the house?"

Jeff.

He stepped into the moonlight, away from the tree where he had been standing, hidden from her sight. How tall he is, she thought . . . how handsome he is becoming, trading the lanky boy-look for a man's muscles . . . it is all the tree felling and house building that is doing it. . . .

Tina realized that she had not spoken to the shy young man who stood, awkwardly waiting for some word from her.

"Oh, Jeff, I am glad it is you. For a moment my heart stopped, thinking it might be animals or Indians."

But why is it pounding like this now, she thought, when I know I am safe and it is Jeff there in the moonlight? Tina wondered at her feeling of weakness, as though her legs would not hold her. There were butterflies in her stomach, too. What could be the problem? Maybe, she was getting ill.

This was awful.

She saw a tree stump and quickly sat on it, afraid her knees would buckle any minute. Jeff dropped down beside her, sitting on his haunches, as comfortably as if he were in an easy chair.

For a few moments they remained there, not moving, a small tableau in the night light: Tina, her eyes sparkling and body tensed as though ready for flight; Jeff, smiling, watching her.

"I'm sorry I missed supper tonight, Christina." Jeff found his voice first. "I had to go to town to get some supplies for your father."

"But Papa was in town all day," Tina said. "Why did he not get the supplies, Jeff? It is such a long trip for you to walk. I do not understand." Tina's blue eyes wore a puzzled expression. It was not like her father to be thoughtless of another's welfare.

"Tina, you are too smart for me," Jeff replied as he stood up and pulled Tina up with him. "I knew it was your birthday and all about the surprises the family had planned for you. I did not want to be in the way at the family celebration. But I am very happy to see you now, little Tina."

Jeff put his hands on Tina's shoulders and turned her towards him.

"Happy birthday."

He leaned down and kissed Tina on the lips. So gentle, so sweet, the kiss, like a bird's wing brushing across her mouth. And, like a bird, her heart soared skyward, flying with a wrenching joy that she had never before felt.

The kiss was over so quickly, it might never have occurred, had Tina's heart not memorized it. Jeff stepped back, as though afraid of what Tina might be thinking of him for his boldness. What he saw in her face was a wonderment, a joy.

"Come, little Tina, I will walk you home." Jeff's voice betrayed his emotion as he tried to speak in a normal tone, but the sound came out low and husky, not at all like his usual Texian twang.

Wordless, Tina walked beside him. The thoughts and feelings that swirled within her brain and the thing she called her heart were too mixed up and muddled to sort out just then. She wanted to take them all out in the quiet of the night and look at each one, each feeling, as though it were the new bonnet or the new shoes. For new they were, these feelings within her.

What did they mean?

Jeff seemed to sense her confusion and walked dog-gedly beside her, saying nothing. She knew that she should be angry for his taking advantage of her, back there in the moonlight. Somehow, she couldn't. She sensed that, when he kissed her, it was because she had wanted it; that she could have prevented it.

But she hadn't wanted to prevent it, had she? How glad she was that it had happened on her sixteenth birthday! Jeff had made her day completely perfect.

They reached the cabin. At the door, Jeff took Tina's hands in his. He gave her a long, searching look.

"I . . . I hope I have not fretted you tonight, little Tina. I didn't mean to kiss you, it just happened, you lookin' so lovely there in the night and all. Will you try to bear me no malice for it, please?"

Jeff's speech was improving daily, but was influenced a great deal by a Bible-reading preacher who had come to live on the next property and had taken it upon himself to teach Jeff the "proper" way to speak.

Tina smiled. She did not know the word "malice" but she could interpret Jeff's expression, and she knew what he meant, especially about how he thought she looked.

Jeff liked her.

As a woman.

Now she understood what all her strange, uneasy feelings had been these past few weeks. She must be in love with Jeff. *That had to be the answer.*

She reached up and took his serious, worried face between her hands. She had to stand on tip-toe to reach that far, so tall he was. Quickly, before she could change her mind, she pulled his face to hers and gave him a warm, tender kiss, then ran quickly into the cabin.

Jeff stood a long moment, unmoving, then turned and walked to the little lean-to where he slept.

Tina watched him from the darkness of the cabin, the family having long since snuffed the candles and gone to bed. Quietly she tip-toed to her corner and started to undress, her shaking fingers having difficulty with the hooks and eyes on her dress.

"Tina, you are so late returning." Mama spoke softly so as not to disturb Papa and the boys who were sleeping soundly, Papa's snore a soft, steady rumble in the room.

"Yes, Mama, I met Jeff and we talked for a while. He is very nice, Jeff, don't you think, Mama?"

"*Ja*, Tina, very nice. For an *Amerikaner*. Now, go to sleep. Such a day this has been, and there is much work to do tomorrow." Mama's voice was soft and sounded as if she were thinking of long-ago times.

Maybe of *her* sixteenth birthday and all that it had meant to her, Tina thought, as she crawled into her bed. She lay, looking into the darkness and savoring the memory of her birthday . . . of Jeff . . . and, most glorious of all, of her *first kiss*.

11

Papa's decision to go to Sisterdale to see about support for a school in In-dustry came about suddenly. His determination, no matter how Mama objected, to take Tina with him was equally out of character for Papa and a source of great delight for Tina. She could not believe that despite all the arguments and fussing by Mama, Papa had finally won out. She would soon be on her way to an unknown place with only her father and *Herr* Heinrich Stiffler, a surveyor from San Felipe. He was headed for New Braunfels to look for work and had asked to accompany them that far.

Mama was appalled.

"It is no *gut*," she stormed. "A young woman, barely sixteen, cannot travel alone, unchaperoned, with two men, even if one of them is her father. I will not have it. *Nein*."

Mama spoke, lower now, "Besides, Tina is needed here for the chores and to help me in the house, *ja*."

"Emilie," Papa replied patiently, "this will probably be the last time in Christina's life that she is free to travel to new places and see what some of the rest of the country is all about. I will take the best of care of her, and she will be a great help on the trail, I know this.

"Jeff will stay here, in charge, with the two boys to help and protect you. It is settled, then, *ja*?"

Mama seemed to know when she was defeated. "*Ja*, Max," she sighed and said no more.

Tina, who had heard the late-night conversation from her bed in the corner, gave herself a small hug of delight.

She was really going, then. Papa had promised many months ago that she should go with him and ride horseback, wearing boy's britches so that she didn't have to ride side-saddle.

They would visit New Braunfels and perhaps stay at a hotel there, Papa had said. Then they would ride to the new village of Sisterdale, also called the Latin Colony by some, where several of Papa's professor friends from the university had settled when they fled Germany after the von Scholls.

. . . and so, dearest Oma, I am excited about our journey. Mama is still being very quiet and does not speak of how she feels about Papa's decision, but Papa and I can hardly contain ourselves, so eager to go we are.

The boys are very jealous of me, and I must confess that I will not believe we are really going until we are well on our way.

As for Jeff, he is raging about Herr Stiffler's joining us as far as New Braunfels. I assured him that Herr Stiffler interests me not at all. He is, after all, an old man of thirty or more and has a disagreeable manner and a red face.

Jeff says it does not matter; he wishes I were not going; he could have gone and "been of more help to Herr von Scholl.*" I have to laugh and say that I think he is like the little boys: jealous of my chance to take this trip with Papa. He only turns red and stalks away.*

I do not tell him this, but I will miss Jeff most of all.

We have packed our supplies, and I am getting acquainted with the mare that Papa has bought for me to ride on this long journey. I named her Lisette, after my friend in Oldenburg—a strange name for a horse, I know, but she will be my true friend, too. It is important to be friends with your horse, Papa says. Much depends on her on the trail.

You must not worry about the danger from Indians, Oma. Since the early part of the year when Herr Meusebach made the *agreement with the Comanches to have peace on both sides, neither Indians nor white settlers have broken the treaty. The Indians trust the German people who have never lied to them, they say.*

You know that I can handle the gun now and so am not afraid of any wild animals we might encounter.

I am looking forward to the journey eagerly . . .

Because they were on horseback and not slowed down by lumbering ox-wagons, they could travel forty or forty-five miles a day, depending on the weather and the terrains they were crossing. The first few days saw not much change; the rolling hills were green, and trees edged the riverbanks.

At the end of the first day they reached the hamlet of Columbus. After crossing the muddy, yellow Colorado River on the ferry boat, Tina struggled to get Lisette up the steep bank on the other side. The effort was worth it, she thought as she caught her breath, in order to visit this town.

Columbus was a charming village, with eighteen or twenty frame houses, their wide porches shaded by beautiful old live oak trees. Tina's heart yearned for a house such as these, for her and her family, especially Mama.

Papa counted three stores, two taverns and a smithy. He also learned from the shopkeeper that horse races were held in Columbus with much wagering, sometimes as high as five hundred dollars on a single race. Papa shook his head in bewilderment; a man could buy five hundred acres of good, rich bottomland for that amount of money. Why would he want to risk it on the whim of a horse race?

Tina wistfully dreamed of witnessing such a race, but knew better than to suggest it to Papa.

After Columbus, it was a long ride over a half-obliterated wagon track to the next town, which was called Gonzales. Nights were spent under the stars, with Papa's tent raised only when rain threatened. *Herr* Stiffler turned out to be as dull and uninteresting as he was homely. Tina tried to avoid talking with him as much as possible.

And so the days of the trip passed.

Deer grazed peacefully in the tall grasses of the prairie or at the edge of the post oak forests of the river bottoms. Once they met a group of Texians with ox-wagons hauling cotton to Houston. Papa visited in English with the men as *Herr* Stiffler looked on, disgruntled because he could speak only German and was missing the conversation.

Tina thought, I can understand most of what they say and could join the conversation if I weren't a girl.

Although she wore boy's trousers and kept her long hair pinned up under a wool tweed cap, she dared not speak to the men. Papa had warned her that when several men were present, she must be very quiet and try to be invisible. He did not want any trouble, he said.

Tina contented herself by continuing her letter to Oma . . .

. . . We camp near a farm whenever we can find one, Oma, so that we can get corn for the horses and food for our night's supper. Usually the farmer will sell Papa a bushel of corn for one dollar and a haunch of venison and some cornbread for fifty cents. Herr Stiffler, a disagreeable man, complains of the high cost of this. Papa tells him we are lucky to find people willing to share with us, even though we must pay.

The high point of our trip so far, Oma, was our stay at the inn in New Braunfels, a most desirable town of German people. First, another ferry must take us across the clear, aquamarine Guadalupe River, a beautiful fast-moving water with tiny cascades and waterfalls along its course and, sometimes, so swift it is almost dangerous to cross.

The inn was a white, frame building, similar to the houses we had seen in Columbus, and very pretty. Here I ate a hot supper with no clean-up chores to do afterward and slept, for the first time since we left home, in a real bed.

It made me feel like a lady!

Another good thing about New Braunfels, Oma, was that the

hateful Herr *Stiffler parted with us there. None of us will miss the other, I am sure, since he seemed to dislike us as much as we did him.*

Soon we arrive at our destination—Sisterdale. The village is just beginning, settled by the friends of Papa from the university and other intellectuals from the homeland. These men are called "free-thinkers" because they dare to dispute the way Germany is being run. I believe they are now in the right place to think free: America.

Papa is excited about seeing these men in Sisterdale. They are his kind, not farmers or cattlemen, but professors and philosophers. They love fine music and art and great literature. Papa says they gather together in the evenings and read plays and books aloud. Will that not be a grand experience to hear such?

I will write you of Sisterdale and the "free thinkers," dear Oma, but for now it must be auf Wiedersehen.

Your loving Granddaughter,
Christina Eudora von Scholl

Tina was enchanted with the little community of Sisterdale. The land rose and fell abruptly now, no longer the easy rolling hills of Industry. Jagged rock outcroppings pierced the earth's surface as though trying to escape, and granite cliffs climbed straight out of the ground searching for what? the sun? Gnarled trees, scraggly mesquite, hugged the flinty clay soil and bent apologetically away from the prevailing wind. Mountain goats and the settlers' Saxony sheep scurried about the hard scrabble rock hills, as at home here as they would have been in the Alps.

Twin streams, Sisters Creeks, meandered through the countryside, occasionally spilling crystal waters in small waterfalls as they flowed toward the tempestuous Guadalupe. Huge cypresses lined the edges of the river, like ornamental columns, their bases washed by the clear, running waters.

Tina loved the place.

Papa was as happy with the people of Sisterdale as Tina was delighted with the setting. He had a noisy and tearful reunion with Johann Richter, a former colleague from Oldenburg. *Herr* Richter insisted that Tina and "my old friend, Professor Max," stay with him and his wife. *Frau* Richter welcomed them as though they were long-lost family and had a meal fit for a king on the table before they had been there one hour.

"*Ach*, it is *gut* to have company," she beamed. "I wish that your dear mama could have made the journey, but I understand, *ja*."

"Mama does not like much the horseback riding," Tina answered, wondering why *Frau* Richter thought that an amusing statement as she put back her head and shook with laughter. Her voluminous body rippled in little waves as she laughed. Tina sat, puzzled and fascinated.

"Of course, horseback riding is not for your Mama. She must stay and take care of herself—and of your brothers, too, *ja*?"

Frau Richter wiped her eyes and looked at Tina with a kind smile.

Before Tina could ask *Frau* Richter any questions, Papa came hurrying into the small house which *Herr* Richter had built himself from the gray native stone found everywhere in these hills.

"Come, my Tina, we go to see the school," Papa said, his voice tight with anticipation. Tina had not realized how very much Papa wanted to start the school in Industry, or how much he had missed his fellow professors, for good talk and music.

The trip to the schoolhouse was a short, pleasant walk. Tina caught sight of a doe and her fawn, grazing in an open patch of green tucked between the woods and the sparkling creek. As she and Papa passed within a few feet of them, the doe raised her head, her white-lined ears up in a listening attitude, and looked at Tina as though to say, "Are you a friend? Or should I take my baby and flee?"

Her decision was one of compromise. She turned and walked slowly and gracefully away, her fawn following without concern. Every few steps the mama stopped and looked back at the intruders, as if to say "Oh, are you still there?"

Without ever seeming to hurry she led her little one into the safety of the wooded hills. As Tina caught a last glimpse of their white tails bobbing through the trees, she hoped they had had enough to eat and their fill of water for the night.

The school was all that Papa had hoped it would be. Built of native stone, the building stood high on its foundation and boasted real glass windows and a heavy wooden door.

Wooden floors, even, sighed Tina. *Ach*, it was a lovely school.

As Papa and *Herr* Richter talked busily of curriculum and books, of teachers and school supplies, Tina fingered some of the books she found on a shelf near the teacher's desk.

One tiny volume, a book of medicine, was entitled, "Facts and Observations on Liver Complaints and Bilious Disorders in General." The author was John Faithorn, MD, and the date of the old book was 1820. Tina read a few pages.

Dr. Faithorn seemed to think every ailment of the body had something to do with the liver. He had, he said, cured people of all manner of illnesses, from headaches to lung congestion, by his special method. Part of this treatment involved temperance in all food and drink, lots of clear spring water taken after each meal, and warmth and dryness of the feet.

Tina read avidly, wondering if she could find something that would fit Mama's ailment. For by now, she was convinced that her mother was ill. There had been all kinds of indications, which she would have noticed sooner if she had not been so taken up with the plans for the trip.

Mama had said very little the last few days before they left. Tina had heard *Frau* Ernst say, "Emilie, do not worry. Friedrich and I will watch over you as though you were our very own, *ja*."

Frau Richter said that Mama must "take care of herself," adding a word about the boys as an afterthought. What did it all mean?

She searched the tiny book on liver ailments for an answer, but it told her nothing. She yearned to be on their homeward journey, the joy of the trip having fled with her suspicions about the state of Mama's health.

"Come, Tina, come," Papa called from outside the schoolhouse. "We are ready to leave, and you still have your head in a book."

"Yes, Papa."

Tina put the tiny volume back in its place and walked slowly toward the door. She knew her father had no notion that his wife might be ill, or he would never have started on their long journey. For this reason, she must not let him guess that she worried about Mama. She must act the same as always.

Smiling at her father as she closed the door behind her, she blinked into the sun. "Papa, it is *gut*, the school, is it not?"

She remembered they had agreed to speak only English on this trip. "I hope we can have such a school at home, Papa. I would like very much to study in this school."

"Yes, Christina, the school is a fine one," Papa said wistfully. "I fear that it will take much more money than we can find to start such a school in Industry. Even though our friends here offer help in the form of books, which we gladly accept, we must have money for other supplies and a place to hold the school.

"*Ach*, Tina, I fear it is a hopeless dream I have, to start the school."

"No, Papa, we will make your dream come true. Somehow, the money will find its way to us. You will see. Is this not America? Do not dreams come true in this land?"

"Yes, my daughter, but only if you make them do so. Nothing is given for nothing. There must be hard work, dedication.

"We shall see what we shall see. I promise you that I will do my best to find the funds we need to get the school started.

"Now, come, we go to a party tonight. *Herr* and *Frau* Kettlemann, from near here, invite us to meet all the neighbors at their home. Are you not glad you brought a dress with you, after all? Who knows, there might be a young man who would see what a beauty my daughter is and fairly swoon to meet her!"

"What fun, Papa! I am glad for the party, but, afterwards, can we start for home? I yearn to see the brothers and Mama."

"Homesick, Tina? *Ja*, I, too. That is *gut*, good to love our home and family."

Tina was convinced that Papa had no worries in his mind about Mama's health. For this she was grateful.

But it was time for them to get back to Industry. Right after the party. . . .

BERTHE and Otto Kettlemann warmly welcomed
Tina and Papa, the Rich-
ters who had brought them and some twenty or twenty-
five other guests into their large log home.

Herr Kettlemann did not wear the look of a sage philoso-
pher, as Papa had described him. He was a rotund little
man, his pink, bald head shining above twinkling blue
eyes which seemed to see all things at once beneath
creamy-white bushy eyebrows. A beard, whiter than the
eyebrows, fell in a deep point below his waist and was
tucked neatly into his wide belt.

To keep it out of the soup, probably, thought Tina with a
smile at the mental picture.

Herr Kettlemann looked like an oversized druid, one of
the elves that protect your house from fires and disasters.
Tina wanted to pick up the little man, whom everyone
called "Uncle," and take him home with her.

His wife, Berthe, was at least a foot taller than her husband, and as Papa said later, "two ax-handles wide." Her
beaming countenance radiated good cheer, and Tina could
not remember feeling so welcome in another's home.

She looked around and was as astounded by the interior
of the house as she had been at the appearance of the host
and hostess.

Papa had said that Otto Kettlemann, a cultured, schol-
arly man, had been a well-known professor of science and

philosophy in Germany. His home displayed a collection of oddments the like of which Tina had never seen. Deerskins covered a huge bed in the corner of the large front room. Snakeskins were stretched across the bed to dry. On the wall hung several guns, both German and American makes.

"It is a passion with Uncle, the hunting," explained *Herr* Richter, as Papa and Tina gazed at the collection.

An oil painting of the Madonna was strangely out of place among the firearms. Antlers, some quite large, held the couple's clothes, several garments hanging from each point, to keep them in balance.

A bookcase, crammed full, held books in the top half, but was filled, in the bottom, with sweet potatoes. Books were everywhere, stacked on top and under the tables. Mixed helter-skelter with the books were a barometer, whisky bottles, powderhorns and specimens of Saxony wool.

It was a hodge-podge of the gentleman's life, and Tina was entranced.

"Come, come, Christina, meet all our neighbors," *Frau* Kettlemann urged Tina, who had found herself a bit shy among all these strangers.

They were not strangers for long. The beer steins were raised in salute to the visitors and long draughts drunk. Two of the older men started to play the fiddle and an "oompa-horn," as Fritz always called the tuba. Old German melodies filled the air, and there was much singing and toasting.

In the dining room (Tina was overwhelmed by the size of the house, with a real room just for eating—what would Mama say?) the tables groaned with food. Turkeys, hams, venison and even lamb were in abundance and all manner of vegetables and side dishes, some of which Tina had never tasted.

"Those are *frijoles*, pinto beans cooked in the Mexican manner," explained *Frau* Kettlemann. "Taste, they are *gut*, although perhaps a bit hot, with the *jalapeño* pepper."

Tina swallowed and gasped as the burning fumes of the hot peppers rose in her throat. She drained her glass of warmish beer, which Papa had offered her, to put out the fire that was raging inside her mouth.

"*Ja*," she managed to gasp to *Frau* Kettlemann, who was holding her sides in laughter at Tina's efforts to stay calm and poised, despite her discomfort. "Very good, the *frijoles, Frau* Kettlemann. But I think I will perhaps rather have some *sauerkraut*, please. It reminds me of the homeland."

With that excuse, Tina abandoned all thought of learning to eat anything cooked in the "Mexican manner."

As she stood nursing her burnt tongue and throat with large swallows of the cold *sauerkraut*, she noticed on the wall of the dining room a clock, very similar to her Oma's clock.

"*Frau* Kettlemann," she began timidly, "that is beautiful, your cuckoo clock. It came from Germany?"

"*Ja*, Christina. It is my pride and joy. Just the other day an *Amerikaner* stood here in this very room and offered me fifty dollars for that clock! Can you imagine such a thing?

"I told him to use his fifty dollars to buy some farmland, eighty acres he could probably get or perhaps a hundred. But he just laughed and said he had land, plenty of it. What he wanted was my clock. Of course I refused, but so persistant he was, he will be back to ask again, he said.

"I am glad you like the little clock, Christina. It means a great deal to me, and I would never wish to part with it."

Tina understood only too well how *Frau* Kettlemann felt about her clock. But inside her mind, a swirling question raged.

If she sold her Oma's clock to the *Amerikaner*, would not Papa have enough money to start the school he so yearned for?

Fifty dollars!

That was more money than Tina had ever seen in her life. She could send the clock to *Frau* Kettlemann to keep safe until the *Amerikaner* came back. Than, with the fifty dollars and the books Papa had received from his friends here, they would have plenty to get a building and supplies and even hire a teacher to help Papa.

Tina's face clouded over.

How could she do it?

Oma's clock. She had not been able to sacrifice it even for Mama whom she loved. Could she give it up for Papa's school?

No . . . *Nein* . . . It was too much to ask of her. She could not let go the last thread that bound her to Oma, the only tangible proof she had that little Oma existed in the faraway land that was becoming dim in her thoughts already. She couldn't let her memory of Oma dim like that; the clock was there to remind her every hour of the grandmother who loved her more than anyone on earth.

Tina's heart was heavy. She looked at the clock, ticking merrily as the party went on. Music grew louder with each passing minute and feet stomped to the rhythms of the old German tunes. Voices were raised in drinking songs and toasts to one another, as everyone got into the spirit of the evening.

She watched from the dining room as *Herr* Richter climbed upon a bench and read aloud from a slip of yellow paper on which he had scrawled some words:

"The tipple, the topple, down cellar it went,
Everything here must be used and spent;
The coat and the button, the boot and the shoe,
The devil will take us, barefooted, too."

Loud laughter rang through the house. *Herr* Richter looked flustered, grinned and tucked the paper in his shirt pocket. Even Tina, as desolate and guilty as she felt, had to smile.

She tried to throw off her despondency and join in the fun of the party.

Just then, one of the men burst into the house from the yard where he had gone to get something from his wagon. He was drenched to the skin.

"*Ach*! The rain has started. In sheets it is coming down, and the wind is coming with it. A norther is on its way, or I miss my guess!" He shook his dripping hat on the floor and stamped his feet. "We should go home, all, before the storm gets too bad, *ja*?"

"*Nein*, my friend," Uncle cried, his pink scalp shining rosy in the lamplight and his beard floating as he moved. Before he continued he tucked it back into his belt. "There is no danger. Stay, the evening is yet young and there is much more *Schnaps* for all."

Everyone went on with the party, enjoying themselves as people do who work very hard in their daily lives. The sound and fury of the sudden storm when it hit was deadened by the sound and fury of the singing, shouting group of free-thinking Germans far from home.

Tina sought out Papa, who sat in a corner of the big room, in deep conversation with a young man, Wolfgang Ehrhart by name, who sat concentrating on Papa's every word and speaking deferentially to "*Herr* Professor."

At that moment, Tina saw her dear Papa with *Herr* Ehrhart's eyes: a distinguished professor of philosophy from the university in Oldenburg, Germany. Not now the poor immigrant, inexperienced in the ways of a strange land, who barely could shoot the flintlock and who had difficulty felling a four-inch tree. Papa now commanded, and received, the respect due one in his profession.

"Papa?" She hated to interrupt this happy moment for her father.

"Excuse me for but a moment, Wolfgang," Papa said with a smile beamed at her. "You have met my daughter, Christina?"

The young man nodded, stood and took Tina's hand. Bowing low, he pressed his lips briefly to her hand. Tina looked down in confusion. No gentleman had ever before kissed her hand.

She found herself wondering what Jeff would think of the old European custom of kissing a lady's hand. She suppressed a giggle. Jeff would think it the silliest thing he had ever seen, she was sure of it.

Acknowledging *Herr* Ehrhart's greeting, Tina turned to her father.

"Papa, the storm is getting worse. Do you not think we should perhaps be going back to *Herr* Richter's house? No one seems to be taking any notice of the rain which is pouring into the cracks around windows and doors and has started to come onto the floor."

"Come, Tina, we will talk to Uncle about it. Yes, you are right; we should be going."

Papa stood up and took his leave of *Herr* Ehrhart, who bowed to him and Tina in farewell.

By now, the water was rushing under the bottom log of the house, undercutting the dirt floor and getting every moment deeper and deeper.

The revelers seemed scarcely to notice. Without missing a beat of the oompah, they climbed up onto chairs, benches and tables, singing, laughing and heedless of the inconvenience.

Tina saw *Herr* Ehrhart leave the house. Scarcely had the heavy door swung closed behind him when he came crashing through it again.

"Uncle, Professor, everyone, listen! The horses . . . Indians have stolen most of the horses! There are only a half-dozen left in the yard, and I could hear the Indians laughing and hooting in the distance. They must have been a small gang of renegades, not to have taken all the horses.

"Come, we must follow them to get our horses back, *ja*?" Momentary stillness filled the room, almost as deafening in its suddenness as the raucous noise of a moment before. Then a stirring seemed to flow through the crowd, and somone shouted, "*Ja*, let us go after them!"

Uncle jumped up onto the nearest table, waving his arms in the air, pulling his beard from its anchorage in his belt and causing it to fly about in cadence to his movements.

"*Nein*, my *gut* friends. Why should we rush out into the

worst of the norther, rain and wind and darkness, when the horses' tracks have been washed away already?

"Let us, instead, continue the evening's entertainment and finish our *Schnaps*. In daylight, we follow the villains by other means I know, besides hoof prints, *ja*?"

No one was eager to set foot out on such a night; all responded with "*Ja*, Uncle, that is what we will do. In morning, is better, *ja*."

And the party continued as though nothing had happened. . . .

September 25, 1847
Dear Oma,

Before I forget the details, I must finish telling you of the experience we had in Sisterdale. I call it The Indian Horse Theft Adventure!

As I told you in my last letter, everyone agreed with Uncle about waiting for morning to track the Indians. That is where I had to stop, I think, to get the letter on the post that goes through Sisterdale.

*Well, to continue: Since **Herr Richter's** horse was one of those stolen—Schatzie and Lisette were still safe in the pasture, hob-*

bled under a mesquite tree—we must stay the night and join in the search for the stolen horses in the morning.

A gray, sullen dawn finally arrived, the light barely penetrating the blanket of thick fog that enveloped everything. It was difficult to find our horses to saddle them and join the others.

Papa did not much like for me to join the hunt for the Indians, but he finally relented after I begged and begged to go. (We will not tell Mama that I did so; she would be furious with Papa.)

We rode single-file; the paths sometimes become very steep and narrow here. The leader, Wolfgang Ehrhart, told each to watch the tail of the horse ahead of him and stay close behind so that no one would get lost.

What a hunting party we were, Oma. I still wore my second-best dress, muddy and bedraggled now, and so I must ride side-saddle. Most of the men had been professors and, like Papa, wore black wool broadcloth suits and tight-collared white shirts. One old gentleman, I forget his name, wore a white linen suit that must have boasted the most wrinkles of any garment in the world!

The funniest sight, which made even Papa laugh—although he says we should never laugh at anyone else's expense—was the tallest man in the company. He sat straight as a ramrod in the saddle, his black wool suit soaking wet and clinging to his bony frame, and, Oma, a high silk hat perched atop his head!

Every time he approached a tree with low hanging branches, he knocked off the top-hat and must dismount and retrieve it, remount and put the top-hat back upon his head. Once more, the entire procedure at the next low limb we passed. No one said a word to him although he did slow the party down in the pursuit of the Indians.

By late morning several people were beginning to get discouraged. We had found no sign of the Indians in the thick fog. The special Indian-hunting method Uncle had boasted of the night before turned out to be only a trick he had used to keep us from rushing out into the storm.

Just as we were about to turn back, someone spied fresh tracks and, with a hoot and a holler, we were off once more on the chase.

For more than an hour we followed those tracks, all riders keeping their eyes and ears open for sign of the horse thieves.

A shout from the front of the line stopped everyone. Herr Ehrhart's *voice rang out.*

"I see something on the trail ahead. I will go and investigate, while you wait for me, ja?"

I, for one, was glad to take a short rest. Ahead we could make out the forms of the others, dismounting and taking a stretch. Then, another shout from Wolfgang rang out in the fog.

"Friends, listen to me," he cried. "We have been deceiving ourselves. What I found on the trail ahead was this slip of yellow paper, the poem that Herr Richter *recited to us only last night at the party!*

"How could it have gotten there, you ask? I will tell you, my friends. We have been following our own tracks, going in a large circle, around and around!"

Now, Oma, I come to the part of the story that makes me love my German heritage. Instead of bewailing the long hours we had been riding in the fog and cold, or crying because the horses obviously were lost forever, this little band of ill-dressed, ill-advised and ill-trained settlers, Germans all, began to laugh and laugh and laugh!

The joke was on them, but they did not care. When you hear a gut *joke, you laugh, ja?*

Even if the joke is on you.

And so, we ended our stay in Sisterdale. For me, it was an adventure I shall always remember, and think about when I am old. I hope that I, too, can always laugh and laugh at a gut *joke!*

Your loving,
Christina Eudora von Scholl

OCTOBER 9, 1847

Dear Oma,

Papa and I have returned safely from our trip to Sisterdale. The journey home was uneventful except for seeing the beautiful spectacle of a prairie fire.

This was an experience to be remembered. We had come more than half-way, having no difficulties in the bright, fall weather, cooler now and blue, blue skies every day.

Late one afternoon we spotted smoke far on the distant horizon. We had made camp on the edge of the prairie under a clump of mesquite trees, the horses munching on the thick grass. The prairie extends for miles in all directions in this area of Texas until it reaches the rich Brazos River bottom with its forest of trees.

As we watched, sparkling flames of scarlet and gold danced in a line at least a mile long, moving slowly, then faster, here in this direction, there in that. The strip of flame, like a diamond necklace, lit the dusk with its brilliance. The prairie fire kept Papa and me entertained for hours before we could go to sleep.

Papa said it was lucky for us it was so far away. "And that the wind is not strong. For I have heard," he added as we sat together in companionship, "of how difficult it is to fight these fires which often threaten homesteads and peoples' very lives."

"But, Papa," I asked, "how do they fight the fires? What can one do, without water, to put out a fire?"

"They round up everyone they can find to help and then all

bring corn-sacks with which they beat the flames until they are extinguished. Sometimes, the winds are so high the flames jump the dead sections and fly along as fast as a man can ride on the speediest horse. This is when the prairie fire becomes truly dangerous.

"But, when, as tonight, it is little wind and the fire is far away, is it not the most amazing sight, my Tina, you have ever seen?"

"Yes, Papa, it truly is," I replied. "Now that the sun has set, the fire is even more spectacular. Look, there, how it shimmers as it dances across the horizon.

"It is like something alive," I told Papa. What I did not tell Papa, Oma, was how happy I was to be sharing this vision of beauty with my father. Just the two of us. It was a moment I shall treasure always.

When we arrived home three days after the prairie fire, Mama, the boys and Jeff were waiting for us, wondering whether we had done well for the school. Papa assured them that we had had a memorable and safe trip, and ja! we had done some good for the school also.

"My old friend, Wolfgang Ehrhart, from the university—you remember him, Emilie?—has given us all these books which made Schatzie's burden much heavier on the way home. Only the promise of extra oats kept her on the trail," Papa said with a pinch for Fritz's cheek and a pat on Wilhelm's head.

"Papa, you tease us," Fritz said. "Schatzie could not understand such a promise. Could she?"

Papa, with the straightest face, assured Fritz that ja, she could and had understood, or else why would she be so happily eating oats out there in the yard at this very moment?

Papa likes to tease Fritz.

Everyone laughed and we all agreed that it was good that we were home again. And so, it is back to chores and everyday living, except that Papa's enthusiasm for the school will keep us excited and busy for some time, I would imagine, Oma. . . .

Papa could not wait to get ready for the new school.

Even without the money for a building, or extra teachers, he planned to go ahead and take each need and problem as it presented itself. The books he had brought back from Sisterdale would help get them started, and, for the time being, Tina could help teach the little ones.

Tina was delighted at the prospect of helping Papa teach the children at the school. Temporarily the Ernsts' big barn behind the hotel would serve as the schoolhouse. *Frau* Ernst, when Papa told her of all he hoped to accomplish there, hurried around to all the neighbors and gathered tables, straight chairs—some with their cowhide seats torn out, but a board across would do nicely—and extra oil lamps.

"*Ach*, Christina," Mama said crossly when Tina came home from the "schoolhouse" late in the afternoon, weary from cleaning and straightening the big area which Papa would use for the school. "*Ach*," she repeated to make sure that Tina heard the vexed tone in her voice. "Always at the school you are, no time for Mama or the home chores anymore, *ja?*"

"Mama," Tina protested, "that is not so. I will do all my chores, milk Daisy, feed the chickens and help with the supper. Do not worry. It is just that Papa needs me. . . ."

"Oh, *ja*, Papa needs you. But do not forget that your real place is here beside me, helping with the home and cooking. Do not get fancy ideas, Tina, about being a schoolteacher for always."

Tina wondered if her mother did not wish that she, too, could spend her days in the Ernsts's barn, covered with cobwebs and manure, but sharing Papa's dream as he worked to make it real.

A letter arrived from Oma, and Mama's thoughts turned from the school back to her home and the things she wanted most: nice furniture and rugs, china and bedding. Her eyes shone as she saw the money fall from the envelope.

"For the house, to replace some of the things you lost in

the fire," Oma's letter explained. She also told Mama that she was shipping some furniture and a trunk of linens and china.

"The man who packed them for me says it may take a year or more before you receive these things," Mama read aloud from Oma's letter. "I hope you can manage until they get there. I wish you were not so far away, just now, my daughter. . . ."

Tina thought she could hear her grandmother's voice speaking through the pages of the letter. Or, perhaps, Mama's voice was beginning to sound a little like Oma's. Perhaps.

She glanced at her clock, pendulum swinging merrily back and forth, back and forth. She wished that Oma herself could come, with the furniture, and stay with them forever.

Mama's voice had a lilt in it that Tina had not heard since before the Ernsts's party. She sounded as though she had something to look forward to again.

"*Ach*, if it is a year, what matters? I can wait, if I know they are coming, the furniture and the lovely things. I can wait."

14

"C-A-T. Cat."
In a stilted voice, not like his usual slow drawl, Jeff laboriously spelled out the simple word. Tina sat next to him on the riverbank, listening as he worked at the lessons she had given him to learn. It was a new, difficult relationship for the two: Tina the teacher, Jeff the student. Always before, Jeff had taught Tina—to build the cabin, to track a 'possum, all the homely things at which he was expert.

At first, he had not wanted to admit that he could neither read nor write. But Papa's enthusiasm for learning and Jeff's own interest in the preparations for the school had finally convinced him to confess his lack of education.

"I . . . ah . . . we had no money for books and such, back in Tennessee," Jeff told Tina with embarrassment. "My ma wanted to send me to a school in the next county, but there was no way to do it. Pa said it didn't matter—I was just goin' to scratch out a livin' on the farm and didn't need no learnin'.

"When we come to Texas, there was no more talk of school. They needed me too much with the work of clearin' the land and buildin' the house and such.

"Then Ma and Pa were both took with the fever, year before last it was. I just went to Houston to look for work. I finally met you and your family and your papa hired me to drive the wagon."

"Oh, Jeff, I never knew about your mama and papa. I am so sorry," Tina said with compassion.

Then, "It will not be long before you will be reading any book on Papa's shelf, Jeff. You are smart . . . do not be discouraged . . . you will write and read before the year is out," she said with a smile.

They sat side by side, Jeff's red head bent over the primer and Tina's brown hair tied up in a ribbon, loose tendrils moving in the breeze on the sunny November day.

A norther had come through Industry the previous week, but this day was beautiful, so they had taken advantage of the mild temperature and sunshine by coming to the river. It was Tina's favorite spot to think and dream. But, for now at least, it was only Jeff's lessons that she must think about.

"You are doing well, Jeff," she said. "Soon it will be easier. Please believe me."

"I don't know, Tina. It seems to come awful slow." Jeff's blue eyes were troubled as he gazed into Tina's sympathetic face. "I feel like such a dunce, sitting in the school seat beside small Fritz, who can already read and write. Maybe I should give it up. Do you really think there is any hope for me at all?"

"Of course, I do, Jeff. See, you have already covered six pages of the primer. Next week we will start on longer words that do not make you feel the baby, *ja*? Please, please, do not give up. You will love it, the reading, when it comes easily for you, I promise."

Impulsively, Tina leaned forward and put her hand over Jeff's. As she did so, she felt the blood rush to her brain, making her feel faint. From a touch of the hand? How could it be so?

Without another word, Jeff lifted Tina to her feet and, taking her chin in his hand, raised her face to look at him.

"Do you have any idea how sweet you are, Tina von Scholl?" he asked in a husky voice. "Or how much you mean to me? Someday . . . when I have become worthy . . . we will talk of the future, '*ja*,' my little Tina?"

Smiling at the flustered girl, Jeff leaned down and kissed

her, first gently on the cheek and then, when she made no move to back away, boldly on the lips.

She caught her breath as Jeff released her, his eyes watching her closely. She smiled at him, wanting to tell him how she felt, and yet, somehow, not quite able to do so. Would he think her too bold, if she told him she loved his kisses and felt the same way about him as he seemed to feel about her? She couldn't. It would be too . . . forward. Wouldn't it?

Jeff broke the silence between them.

"Are you angry, Tina? To have such a dumb-ox as me to think he has the right to kiss you?"

"*Ach*, Jeff," Tina started to reply in German, so agitated she felt, first by the kiss and now by Jeff's words. Switching quickly to English, "Jeff, you must not think of yourself so unkindly. You are a good person. Because you do not read or write makes no difference as to how I feel about you, or how you should feel about yourself.

"I . . . I am not angry," she said, suddenly shy. "I . . . liked . . . it, the kiss."

No more could she say, but Tina knew that from this moment there would be a different feeling between them and, as Jeff had said earlier, maybe someday . . . .

"*Jeff, Tina*! You must come home now! Papa has sent me to find you." It was Will, red-faced from running.

"What is it, Will? What does Papa need that you should lose your breath running all the way to the river?" Tina felt her heart constrict with a tiny fear. Mama?

As though Will read her thoughts, he said, "It is Mama, Tina. She has taken to her bed and does not get up. Sometimes she moans, but otherwise speaks no word to us. Papa says we must all hurry to Industry and get *Frau* Ernst and the doctor to come see Mama. We must stay, all of us, at the hotel until he sends for us.

"What can be the matter, Tina, with Mama?" Will's voice had a tight edge of worry in it. "Do you think she has the fever and will die, like Jeff told me about his parents?"

"No, of course not, Will." Tina spoke crossly, not wanting to hear any of her own thoughts spoken aloud, for fear of making them become reality.

Quickly Jeff gathered up books and papers, and they started back toward the cabin, running, then walking to catch their breath, then running again.

As they approached the little house, Tina sent an unspoken prayer heavenward, "Let her be all right, please, God."

. . . so you see, dearest Oma, why it was with such happiness and joy that we learned, when we returned home from Industry on the following day, that we had a new baby sister, and that Mama was fine!

Her name is Louisa Emilie—in honor of **Frau Ernst** *and, of course, Mama—and she is the tiniest, pinkest mite of a baby I have ever seen. My heart is so full of thankfulness that it was a baby, all of Mama's sicknesses these past few months, and not the fever.*

I cannot tell you how surprised we all were. It had never crossed my mind that Mama might ever have another baby. She never said a word to me about it, and, dressed always, since the party, in those loose jackets. Who could have guessed the truth?

Papa is beside himself with joy and pride, and the boys think it is wonderful to have a younger sister with whom they can play, but who will not be "so bossy as Tina."

I understand now a lot of things which have puzzled me these past few months, Oma. I wish Mama would have talked to me about the baby. I could have helped her more than I did and understood when she seemed extra cross or unhappy.

Why cannot Mama and I talk to each other about the things that mean the most to us, Oma? You and I could always speak with ease. I wish so much for that with Mama, but she never lets me come that close to her.

Is it something wrong that I do, Oma?

Next to the excitement about Louisa—she is such a darling, I wish you could see her—nothing seems worth the writing.

Papa's school is coming along handsomely. Thirteen pupils he has so far, and all doing well. There is talk that some of the people here will donate money for a building soon, so that we do not have to stay in the Ernsts's barn, sharing space with the horses and cows. Would not that be lovely?

Mama calls for me to come get Louisa, who has finished her feeding. I am glad that I can help Mama, she is still very weak.

Your loving,
Christina Eudora von Scholl

. . . "Take Louisa, Tina, and put her in her cradle. Then, come back and sit beside me for awhile, *ja?*" Mama's voice was soft and gentle, the shrillness that Tina was so used to hearing gone from it.

Carefully taking the tiny baby from her mother's arms and placing her in the homemade cradle—when had Papa found time to make the little bed?—Tina returned to her mother's side.

"*Ja*, Mama?" she said as she sat down beside her mother.

"I am sorry that I did not tell you of the baby coming, my Tina," Mama said as she took Tina's hand in hers. "I had much fear and unhappiness in me, to have this baby in a strange and foreign land. I could not speak of it, to you or anyone. Papa thought I should tell you, to explain, and I wanted to; but the words would not come. Will you forgive me?"

"Mama, there is nothing to forgive. I was so worried about you, about your health. And now, what joy, to know it was little Louisa all the time!"

Tina's eyes shone with happiness, about her baby sister and, even more, about Mama speaking to her in the loving way she was doing now. It was her dearest wish come true . . . for the two of them to have a better understanding of one another . . . to be friends.

"*Ach*, that is *gut*, Tina. You are a good daughter." Mama's eyes grew damp. "I wish that I had been such a daughter to my mama, your Oma. We might have been happier, she and I, if I had not been so aloof, so cold. I wish I could make it up to her; but, at least, I will try to make it up to you, Christina."

Her mother paused and then went on, more hesitantly. "I know that you have felt . . . that I have loved the brothers more than I loved you, *ja? Nein, nein,* is not the truth. But the boys seemed to need me more than you did. You seemed only to need your grandmother and your papa, is it not so?"

Mama looked keenly at Tina, waiting for words from the girl to tell her what she wanted to hear.

"Oh, Mama, *no!*" Tina cried, throwing herself into her mother's arms. "I love you, Mama. I only turned to Oma and Papa—although I love them both dearly—because I thought you did not love *me!*"

Mama smoothed Tina's hair and crooned a little humming sound that she used with Fritz—and now, with Louisa—to calm them when they were upset.

"Tina, we have waited almost too long, as I did with your Oma, to find that we love and need each other. I want you to promise that you forgive me, and that we will never drift apart again. Will you do that for me, my daughter?"

"*Ja,* Mama, *ja,* I promise. And, now," Tina said with brisk authority as she rose from the bed and smoothed the quilt, "now the patient must rest. I will watch the baby and get the supper. Sweet dreams, Mama."

"Thank you, Tina. I am tired. It will feel good to rest. . . ." Mama's voice trailed off as she sank into a deep, peaceful slumber.

I never thought there was this much happiness in all the world, thought Tina as she washed the baby's tiny garments in the river. The day was unseasonably warm, and she was taking advantage of it to get some much-needed family laundry done. Soon the river would be too cold for washing clothes, and she would have to haul water to the house, heat it over an open fire in the big copper wash kettle and then stand outside in the cold, damp air with her arms to their elbows in soapy water. She much preferred the river.

Her heart was so full of gladness these days it felt as though it would burst. Delight in the baby, Louisa Emilie, and the daily changes in her tiny form; joy in her new relationship with Mama, who laughed with her when Louisa tried to smile and sometimes talked for hours about her own childhood and feelings when she was growing up; and, especially, her growing tenderness for Jeff.

There had been no opportunity for another encounter such as the one by the river on the day that Louisa was born. Nevertheless, Tina could tell by the light in his eyes as he looked at her that Jeff's feelings had not changed.

How can everything be so wonderful for me? she wondered. All my fondest dreams seem to be coming true. Do I deserve all of this? Will it be always so? These were questions she could not answer. Difficult questions. Only time would have the solution . . . but for now, she reveled in happiness. Each day brought a new merriment, a new delight.

She lingered by "her river." So many hours had she spent in this peaceful place, watching the clear waters flow along, like the hours on her little clock. There was neither beginning nor ending to either of them, just a circle of movement and time, like her life had become, day after day of busy, happy hours. Suddenly a chill swept across her face. The breeze had shifted and become a stiff wind from the north. The temperature started to drop, swiftly, and Tina hurriedly gathered her freshly washed clothing into the basket and started at a trot for home.

A norther! Only the second of the season, it could bring with it freezing rain and chilled days and nights, enough to cause much misery for those unprepared for it.

Scattered droplets of rain had already begun to splash against her back as she hurried along, lugging the basket of heavy, wet clothes. Colder, already, it was, at least fifteen degrees in the past fifteen minutes. She pulled open the heavy door of the log house and stopped just inside, trying to catch her breath.

"What is it, Tina?" Mama asked wearily from the bed where she was nursing Louisa.

"A norther, Mama," Tina answered as she started hanging the wet clothes over every available chair or hook in the house. It would take a long time for them to dry, now that the warm air was gone.

"*Ach*, I was hoping to get a chance to go outside a bit, before the winter weather sets in," Mama said. "I remember those northers from last January when we first came here, *ja*?"

Mama had been up from her bed very little since the birth of Louisa. *Frau* Ernst said that she was run down and needed extra rest. Tina had doubled her efforts to take good care of Mama and Louisa—and the boys and Papa.

She ran outside to the woodpile and brought logs into the house. She took kindling, small branches gathered by the boys, and laid the fire in the stone fireplace which Papa and Jeff had spent many weeks building. Tina was grateful that it was completed and ready for this cold weather. Mama and Louisa must not get chilled.

The logs added, she twisted one piece of precious paper into a brand and lit it with a wooden match. Carefully, she held the burning torch to the kindling, hoping it would catch before the paper burned down to her fingers. She did not want to waste a second match on one fire.

The branches caught with a quick flame and soon the fireplace glowed a warm yellow-orange as the logs began to burn. The warmth reached a few feet into the large room, as the sound of the norther outside drowned out the crackling of the fire.

It was going to be a bad one. Tina hoped the boys and Papa and Jeff would hurry in from the field where they were clearing more land for next year's crops.

She prepared supper, a cold meal because she could not cook outside. Papa would soon have the pot-hanger fixed in place so that she could cook in the fireplace, but now the warmth of the fire could only cheer them. She did put an old iron kettle at the edge of the hearth to heat water for Mama's tea.

For the rest of them, cold meat and sweet potatoes would have to do.

The door flew open and, amidst a gust of cold, wet air, Papa and the boys rushed into the house, Jeff right behind them.

"*Ach*," Papa exclaimed, as he hurried to the fireplace and rubbed wet, cold hands together, "such a night! This is a norther to remember, *ja*. Already the rain starts to freeze as it falls—and this afternoon as balmy as a spring day! I am glad that Jeff and I completed the fireplace in time, *ja*?

"Emilie, how do you feel? And how is my new little *Liebchen*, eh?"

"I am feeling better, I think, Max," Mama said. "Still a bit weak, but with Tina's good broth and tea and pampering, I recover more each day, *ja*?" Mama gave Tina a smile which sent the girl's spirits soaring.

"*Ja*," Papa said, looking at Tina with pride, "Tina is a good nurse. And a good teacher, too. She is getting the littlest ones at the school ready for reading and writing. A very good job she does."

"Thank you, Mama, Papa," said Tina with a smile. Her voice was soft, but the happy beating of her heart was loud, loud, loud.

The norther became a real winter storm, lasting more than a week. Inside the little house a battle raged to keep warm.

The boys and Jeff, who had moved into the house for the duration of the storm, kept the fire box full of wood and sticks. Papa, who prided himself on being the best fire-builder in Texas, kept the fireplace glowing, in the daytime with a roaring fire and at night with banked coals which shone red in the darkness.

They pulled Mama's bed and Louisa's cradle up close to the fireplace so that they could get all the heat possible. Jeff tacked blankets over the drafty windows to keep the raging wind out, and everyone wore all the clothes they could pile on to keep their teeth from chattering.

Their efforts were not too successful. Fritz began sniffling. Will sounded as though he would soon be wheezing. Mama directed Tina to put mustard plasters and throat compresses on both of them, much to their chagrin.

Water became a problem. Papa, Jeff and the boys had to brave the cold, wet gale on periodic trips to the river, laden with buckets and kettles. Then, they must flounder in the ankle-deep muck to reach the rampaging river. Only Jeff and Papa dared this part of the job; the river was too swift for the young boys to handle. At home once more, they warned Tina to use only the smallest amount of water possible to conserve what they had. The boys were delighted that no baths would be taken for awhile.

Louisa seemed to thrive on the cold. Her cheeks were petal pink, and her little rosebud mouth often bloomed into a smile, although Papa insisted that babies her age could not really smile. Mama and Tina nodded at each other, sure that Louisa's "smiles" were just for them.

Mama's weakness worried Tina. It seemed to her that Mama should be up and around now. Louisa would soon be a month old, and still Mama could not get her strength back.

Perhaps when the worst of the bleak, freezing weather was over, Mama would feel better. In the meantime, Tina and Papa conferred about their worries, whispering in the far corner of the room, and the boys kept more quiet than usual, sensing that Mama needed her rest.

Then, one morning Mama had a raging fever. Frightened at her flushed face and the burning sensation of her skin when she placed fingertips on Mama's forehead, Tina called Papa, who had been gathering more branches for kindling. He took one look at his wife, lying so still among the quilts, and his face turned ashen.

"Emilie," he spoke quietly. "Emilie, I go for the doctor. I worry for you, my dear. Please, try to drink some of Tina's broth, and I will be back very soon."

"*Ach*, Max, no," breathed Mama, so softly Papa had to lean down to hear her words. "Do not go out in that storm. You will get sick, and we cannot have Papa sick, can we, children?"

Papa shook his head and glanced at Tina. "Take care of your mama, Tina. I will be back as soon as I can get Doctor Knust."

"*Ja*, Papa."

Tina had difficulty getting out the words, so constricted with fear and worry was her throat.

What if Mama had the fever, the same "virulent fever" that took both of Jeff's parents and many others they had known? It wouldn't matter if Doctor Knust came or not. There was nothing to do for the fever—but pray.

And very few prayers had been answered; most patients died within twenty-four hours.

Tina's fearful thoughts were interrupted by the sound of crying from the little cradle. It was time for Louisa to eat.

Mama is much too ill to nurse the baby, Tina thought. She made a sugar-water solution and dipped a clean handkerchief into it. Then, gently picking up the baby, she held her in her arms in front of the fireplace. Louisa's crying ceased as her head bobbed, looking for sustenance. Tina put the twisted sugar-water cloth into her mouth.

The baby quieted down, and Tina listened to the loud sucking noises as Louisa drew the sugar water from the cloth. A poor substitute for her regular fare, but at least it would keep her satisfied until morning.

Surely, Mama would be better by then.

But morning brought no improvement in Emilie von Scholl's condition.

Dr. Knust had come back with Papa and had examined her carefully. Then he pulled Papa aside and spoke in low tones. Without another look at his patient, he left to brave the storm and drive his wagon back to Industry.

Papa looked stricken.

"Children, Jeff, come here," he said quietly.

Tina, Jeff and the two boys stood before him in an apprehensive little huddle.

"Mama . . . my dear wife . . . has the virulent fever. *Herr* Doctor says there is little that can be done for her. He has six other cases in Industry. The poor man is devastated—so helpless he feels." Papa kept talking now, not knowing what he said, but afraid to look into the eyes of his children.

He knew he would see the truth reflected in them. They were going to lose Mama.

AMA's voice from the bed roused the five who stood as though mesmerized, staring into each other's agonized faces.

Jeff turned and made a big show of putting logs on the fire and stirring it up. He kept blowing his nose into his big, blue handkerchief.

The boys, Tina and Papa moved silently to Mama's bedside. Tina held Will's hand on one side, her arm about Fritz's trembling shoulder on the other. Papa was the first to speak.

"Yes, my *Liebchen*, what is it? Do you need something? What can we do for you?"

"*Ach*, Max, no one can do anything for me, I know this," Mama said calmly. "If I had not already guessed that what has attacked me is the virulent fever, the expressions on your four faces would have given me the truth." She paused to gather strength for what she had to say.

"You must not be sad, my family; my only sadness is that death is coming now when I have just learned how to live. But, I want to leave you something . . . to remember me by, *ja*?"

Papa made a sweeping gesture with his arm. "Emilie, *no*, you will not die. We will fight the fever. How could we go on without you? You are our strength . . . our stability. . . ." Papa's voice broke, and he could not continue.

"Please, Max, let us not waste precious time in pretending. I will not get well. The fever is the master here. We must bow to it . . . and make our peace with each other and with God."

Mama spoke with more strength and assurance now. It was she who comforted and gave courage to them, they who denied the truth of her words. They clung to a straw of yearning hope that the doctor was wrong, that Mama would recover from this dread ailment which was about to tear apart their lives.

"Boys, come close," Mama said, smiling. "Will, you are the eldest son. You must be brave for Fritz and help your sister, Tina, and your father to care for little Louisa, *ja*?"

Will. Mama had called Wilhelm—Will. Tina's mind caught the significance of that small word. Mama had known all along they were calling her eldest son by an *Amerikaner* name!

And now, she too used it to speak to him for perhaps the last time.

As though she realized Tina's dilemma, Mama spoke to Fritz. "And, my little Fritz, is there not a new name for you, too? What about *Fred*? Would not that be a good *Amerikaner* name for you, my sweet one?"

Papa's face reflected the astonishment that Tina was feeling at her mother's words. Mama who hated everything that was not German . . . Mama who now called the boys by new names for their lives in the new world. Had she changed her mind about Texas and America?

"*Ja*, my children," Mama continued, her voice weaker but determined. "I have realized how wrong I was to try to hang on to the old country, the old ways. It is time for the new country, new ways . . . and time for you to become true Americans . . . true Texans, *ja*? I regret now that I refused to learn the English, but I am glad Papa has taught you three children."

As Mama paused to catch her breath, a startled look passed between Tina and Papa. So Mama had known even this?

Tina was beginning to realize what a remarkable woman was her Mama.

She gazed at her mother with new respect, mingled with an aching love, and Emilie von Scholl continued her musings, half to her family, half to herself.

"*Ja*, I have been wrong. But, no more. I want you to become good citizens of this new land and make a name for yourselves. Work hard . . . *Arbeit macht das Leben süß* . . . 'Work makes life sweet.'

"But, a promise I must have, from all of you, *ja*?" Mama's eyes searched each face before her, waiting for and receiving nods from all.

"You must, every one, promise me that, although you will become good Americans in every way, you will not forget your heritage. You are Germans, too, always. Keep alive the old traditions and remember the language . . . never lose the gift you were given at your birth.

"It is possible, I think," Mama said, her voice growing so weak that her husband and children leaned closer to hear, "to keep the faith with both your countries, with both backgrounds that will mean so much to your children and their children. I am sorry I will not be here to see those little ones."

"Mama, Mama," Tina cried, "please do not say so. Please try to rest and get your strength back, *ja*?"

"No, my Christina, I must say what I have to say. Especially, to you and to Papa.

"To you, Tina, my first-born, I must leave the care of Louisa, my last. She is so tiny to be without a Mama . . . but, you will take good care of her and treat her tenderly, I know this. Go now, my darling Tina, I must talk to Papa, *ja*?"

"Oh, Mama, I promise you I will care for Louisa always, if you want me to say it. But, we need you for all of us, not just the baby . . . please. . . ."

But Mama had closed her eyes, gathering strength for the words she wished to say to Papa. Tina backed away, her eyes never leaving her mother's drawn and flushed face.

Papa stood alone by the bedside, Mama's frail hand in his. Tina could hear their words, soft and private as they were, and she locked them in her memory.

"Max, come closer . . . hold me once more. I have not always been what you wanted me to be, Max; often I have failed you. But, always I have loved you, in my own way, *ja.*

"Remember that, dearest Max . . . I have loved you. . . ."

"Emilie, *Liebchen*, please . . ."

. . . And so, dear Oma, we have buried Mama. In the little cemetery on the hillside in Industry, with so many others who came to this new land with such hopes for the future.

I have cried many tears, Oma.

Now, I must think of the future that Mama will never see. She has left me to care for Papa and the boys, and, especially, for little Louisa. I must have courage and carry on, ja?

The Ernsts and all the friends and neighbors here have been wonderful to us. Mountains of food have poured in and everyone tries to bring Papa out of his sadness.

Ann Freulich, a young woman of Industry who has just had a baby, will nurse Louisa until we can get a goat. By then, she should be able to survive very well on the rich goat's milk.

In all our sorrow, the day which the Americans celebrate, called Thanksgiving, has passed us by. The von Scholls have little to be thankful for this year . . . and much.

Mama's last words to us, her legacy, will sustain us and make us better Germans and better Americans, I know this, Oma.

Soon it will be Christmas, our first in America. So hard it will be, without Mama, to be happy at Christmas. But for the little ones, ja, *and for Papa, too, I will try to make Christmas as I remember it from the homeland.*

It will be my promise kept, to Mama.

Christina

IN the days that followed, Tina's sorrow for the loss of Mama had to be set aside, only to be experienced during the long, dark nights. For the boys' sakes, in the daytime, she put on a smile and a cheerfulness she did not feel; it seemed to help them get through this hard time. In the evenings, there was Papa to think of—quiet, thoughtful Papa, smoking his pipe for long, lonely hours before he could go to bed for much-needed rest.

Tina tried to cheer Papa by bringing Louisa and asking him to hold her while she finished supper, or to see how round and rosy the baby was becoming. He smiled at her then, and at Louisa, but his heart was not in it.

It was a grim little household as Christmas fast advanced upon it.

Tina determined that she would make Christmas as happy a time as she possibly could, especially for little Fred—they had adopted Mama's American name for Fritz—who seemed so lost these days without Mama.

Every night after all the chores were done and the boys and Papa were in bed for the night, Tina stayed up an extra hour, rocking Louisa's cradle with her toe as she sat in Papa's chair beside the single candle. She sewed shirts for the boys and for Jeff from the calico given to Mama at the Ernsts' party. Then she knit Papa a long, gray wool scarf, one that would wrap around his throat at least twice and keep him warm this winter. For the wool, she had to unravel two pairs of the socks she had knit on the long ocean voyage to America. Each boy would just have to do without one extra pair of socks.

For her baby sister, she made a delicate long white dress, from one of the fine batiste petticoats which *Frau Ernst* had given her to wear with the lovely yellow party gown. Her eyes grew tired and ached from the hundreds of tiny stitches it took to sew on the rows and rows of lace trim. She wanted the dress to have the finest workmanship she could manage. Louisa must have the best that she could give her. Tina swore to herself that her infant sister would want for nothing . . . losing her mama at such a tender age was enough hardship for anyone to bear.

"Life will be easier for you, little Louisa, then it has been for the rest of us, the boys, Papa and me, easier than it was for Mama," she promised the sleeping baby lying so peacefully in her cradle as it rocked to and fro.

Two weeks before Christmas, as Tina was preparing the evening meal and listening to Will's arithmetic lesson, the heavy door flew open and Jeff and Papa heaved themselves through it, lugging a huge black thing between them. As Tina came to see what was happening, she recognized the "thing" as a cookstove.

Mama's stove . . . how she had yearned for it to arrive from Galveston . . . how excited she would be if—Tina swallowed the lump in her throat as she looked at Papa's expectant face.

"Oh, Papa, it is beautiful, the cookstove!" she exclaimed, her natural enthusiasm rising above her inner feelings. "And just in time for the Christmas baking. Now I can make *Lebkuchen* and, if I can locate some hartshorn crystals, I will make too the *Pfeffernüsse*. You have always loved the pepper nuts, *ja*, Papa?"

"Yes, my Tina," Papa answered as he and Jeff struggled to get the stove in position so that they could cut a hole in the roof for the stove-pipe.

"I always enjoyed the Christmas cookies which your dear mama baked, and Oma, also. But, you have so many burdens on you now, with Louisa to care for and the household work to do, perhaps this year we should forget the holiday. We are in mourning for your mama, you know. Everyone would understand."

"No, Papa, we will have Christmas." Tina spoke with the quiet determination which Papa knew preceded her occasional displays of stubbornness.

"We owe it to the boys to keep things as normal as possible. It will be very hard to do, without Mama, but she would never want us to forget Christmas, never!"

"Ah, Tina, you are growing every day. You will become a fine wife and mother some day. It will be as you say: Christmas for the von Scholls will be sad, but sweet, *ja*? For we have much to be happy about, even in our sadness, is that not so?"

"Yes, Papa, we have each other and Louisa, and the land and America. We will revere our mama's memory; but we will look forward to the lives we will have here.

"I want all of us to grow up as good Americans, never forgetting that we are Germans, too. Is that not what Mama said to us, before she died?"

"You are right, Tina. That is exactly what she wished for us. And we will do it, yes.

"Tomorrow I start looking in the woods by the river for a young cedar. On Christmas Eve I will bring it home, and we will have the *Tannenbaum*."

"Thank you, Papa, for understanding," Tina said with a grateful smile.

Christmas Eve came too fast for Tina, who was working nearly all night now to finish the gifts for her family.

She sent the boys scurrying to find pecans which had fallen from the huge trees near the river. In the evenings, after schoolwork was finished, they sat in front of the fireplace, shelling the nuts. They threw the shells into the fire, sending crackling sparks up the chimney and filling the room with a nutty, woodsy aroma.

The nutmeats were used in the cookies that Tina baked each day in the new stove's ample oven. Jeff often came and stood behind her as she brought out another pan of the fragrant, spicy cookies, filled with pecans, cinnamon, nutmeg and cloves.

"Mmmm," Jeff would say, reaching for a steaming hot cookie.

"No, Jeff, not yet! We must not taste the Christmas cookies until Christmas Eve. It is the custom of my grand-mother, my Oma, who always baked hundreds of these treats for us, starting on the first of December. I, of course, am doing only a few—to have the taste and smells of Christmas in the house. It is too expensive, the sugar, to do more than that."

Jeff grinned and nodded and went on about his business.

"Well," he drawled one day, as he opened the door to leave the warm house, "at least, I can come and smell them, if that's all right with you. *Ja*, Tina?"

Tina could not help but laugh at Jeff's foolishness. But she would not relent—he could smell them, yes, but no tasting, till Christmas Eve.

Finally, the gifts were completed and Tina's horde of sweets carefully stored in tins on the shelf above the stove. The boys were beside themselves with excitement. Papa and Jeff, with their help, were to cut the tree and bring it home this morning.

Tina had cleared a spot for the tree, near the window where anyone approaching the house could see its wel-coming branches.

There they came, the men, dragging the cedar behind them. They pulled it into the house and set it onto the wooden stand that Papa had made from scrap boards left from the roof.

"Ooooh," breathed Tina as she looked at the grand tree, reaching to the roof at that point in the room. "If you had cut a taller one, we would have had to put it in the middle of the house," she laughingly told Papa, who was standing back to admire his choice of Christmas trees.

Jeff plopped down in front of the fire to catch his breath and said, "I knew the German people were differentl, Tina, but this is too much. A tree in the house? This is a custom I can't understand. Why would you bring a cedar tree into the house?"

"Ah, Jeff." Tina smiled as she sat in the rocker to feed Louisa her goat's milk dinner. "I will tell you the story as my grandmother, my Oma, told it to us when we were very little children. Come, boys, sit beside me. You always liked to hear this legend when Oma would repeat it each year, is not this so?"

"Yes, Tina," Will cried with enthusiasm. "It would not seem like Christmas, without the story of the *Tannenbaum*. That's German for Christmas tree, Jeff." Will put on an expression of one who knows much and is willing to share his knowledge with lesser folk.

Jeff grinned.

"There are many legends about the Christmas tree, Jeff," said Tina, as she put Louisa on her shoulder to burp.

"This is the one Oma told us: During the Middle Ages, the Germans celebrated the feast of Adam and Eve and dramatized the story of the Garden of Eden. A fir tree was hung with apples to symbolize Eve's Fall. The next day, Christmas, they would burn pyramid-shaped candelabra which they called, in English, "Lightstocks." After many years the candles from the Lightstock were added to the fir tree. This was the beginning of the Christmas tree, according to Oma who has repeated the story for many, many years after hearing it from her Oma before that. And so on . . ."

"Tell Jeff about *Kriss Kringle*, Tina, please," begged little Fred, who sat on the floor beside Tina's rocker. She knew that he loved to hear the story himself but was using Jeff as an excuse.

"*Kriss Kringle* used to be known as *Christkindl*, the

Christ Child. He it was who brought gifts for German children who had been good," Tina said, with a meaningful glance at Fred.

"*Christkindl* is not really the Christ Child but an angel sent from heaven, wearing white robes and golden crown and having big golden wings. Some people even claim," Tina said with a mischievous twinkle in her eye, "that *Christkindl* is a girl!"

Will and Fred shouted, "Oh, no, it could not be!" and rolled on the floor in boisterous laughter.

Tina drew herself up in the chair and said, with pretended anger, "And just why could not the angel be a girl, eh?"

Jeff sat, enjoying the teasing among the three, and then quietly said, "I remember Ma tellin' me a story once about a jolly old fellow called St. Nick. Is he the same as *Kriss Kringle*, Tina, do you reckon?"

"Yes, I am sure that every country has different stories for Christmastime, Jeff. We will have to learn what is Christmas in America.

"But this year, we will try to have an old-fashioned German Christmas. Even I have asked Papa to buy a goose."

"Roast goose, yummm," said Will, his eyes on the tin of cookies above the stove. "Tina, Mama would be proud of you, I know this."

"I hope so, Will. Oh, I hope so," Tina answered her brother in a whisper.

The tree was trimmed with some of the cookies which Tina had baked; string was attached to fix them on the tree. Candles were too dear, and too dangerous in the log house, to put on the tree as they had in the big library in Oldenburg. But Tina decorated a candle in the center of the table with small cedar boughs and pecans and tiny red ribbons which she found in Mama's sewing basket.

Papa had bartered for some crisp, red apples, which they tied to the tree, to be eaten on Christmas Day. It was a beautiful tree, all agreed, the cedar's fragrant aroma filling the house.

"Come, children, Jeff, it is *Heiligabend*, Christmas Eve, time for the songfest." Papa, after his hesitation about celebrating Christmas, had gotten into the full swing of the preparations and now seemed his usual jovial self.

Tina thought, *He is pretending, for our sakes.* With Papa leading them, Will, Fred and Tina began to sing, Jeff listening in admiration:

"O Tannenbaum, O Tannenbaum,
Wie treu sind deine Blätter."

"O Christmas tree, O Christmas tree,
How faithful are your needles."

Then the two boys, Will and Fred, stood in front of the Christmas tree and sang, their clear soprano voices in harmony:

"Der Christbaum ist der schönste Baum,
Den wir auf Erden kennen . . ."

"The Christmas tree is the fairest tree,
That we on earth can know . . ."

When they had finished, Tina explained to Jeff, "This song is sung by the German children as they stand around the Christmas tree, before receiving their Christmas gifts.

"Come, Fred, you may distribute the gifts which are under the tree, *ja*, Papa?"

"*Ja*, Daughter, and may we perhaps have some of those lovely cookies you have been baking these past two weeks in preparation for this special night?" Papa's eyes twinkled as Tina rushed to the stove and reached the tins of cookies down from the shelf.

"*Ach*, I almost forgot them, the cookies," she said.

"I was fixin' to remind you, Tina, if your papa had not done it first," Jeff said with a grin at Max von Scholl.

"Here, eat," Tina said, as she passed the plate on which she had arranged some of each kind of cookie. "There are plenty more. I hope they as good as Oma's and Mama's."

Her voice took on a worried tone. "It is my first time making them all alone, and with the new cookstove, besides.

"Hmmmm," Jeff said, nodding his head as he devoured a cookie whole.

"Delicious, Tina, I am very proud of you," said Papa. "Now, boys, you may start with the presents. It is good that we have the German Christmas. We must keep the traditions alive, *ja*." Papa nodded his head as he bit into his third *Pfeffernüsse*.

Tina's gifts were accepted with shouts of joy and laughter, each person pleased with what she had made him, especially Jeff. He could not get used to the idea that the von Scholl family was willing to share this special time with him. It was *wunderbar*, he thought, borrowing Tina's favorite German word.

After Papa had exclaimed over the scarf and wound it about his throat to show how it would look, and the boys had tried on their new shirts for Tina to see the fit, after the tins of cookies, once crammed full, held less than a dozen of the sweets . . . only then did Papa bring a small package from the depths of his coat pocket.

"Tina," he said, "this is for you. May you cherish it always, for it is a remembrance of your dear Mama. I want you to have it; you have earned it, my Tina. Mama would say so, I know this." Papa's voice broke as he handed the box to Tina.

She quickly opened the box. It was Mama's garnet cross, the one Opa and Oma had brought her from a long-ago trip to Vienna. Her eyes shining, Tina fastened the clasp of the thin golden chain around her neck.

"Papa, thank you. There is nothing I could have wanted more. I have always loved this cross . . . and I will keep it forever."

At that moment, Louisa decided it was time to eat, Christmas Eve or no. She let out a howl from the cradle and the four people who had become her subjects rushed to pick up the screaming infant.

"*Fröhliche Weihnachten*, little princess," Papa said tenderly as the baby quieted down, "Merry Christmas."

Later that night Tina lay awake, thinking of the day's events and of how happy she felt . . . and how sad.

How can both emotions be this strong inside me at the same time, she wondered. Perhaps, that is the meaning of the word, *bittersweet*, the sad and the happy, blending into one.

She wondered what time it was. Everyone else was sleeping soundly. It was too dark to see Oma's little clock, and she did not want to strike a match. Matches were expensive and often hard to get. "Waste not, want not," Mama had always said.

She could hear the comforting tick and knew that if she waited, the little cuckoo would sing his song, telling her the time.

As she lay in the dark, waiting, she thought of Oma. She would write her grandmother a letter tomorrow, after the roast goose and all that went with it had been consumed, and Papa and the others had fallen into an after-the-feast slumber.

She hoped Oma was happy with Aunt Rose and Uncle Heinrich, and that she would live many more Christmases.

How strange, she thought, that a year ago I was crying for fear that Oma would leave us; and now, Oma is well, and Mama in her grave.

Life is indeed a mystery, she thought, but I want to taste everything it has to offer.

The little door on Oma's clock clicked open, and Tina heard the tiny bird chirp its message. Twelve times it sang its cuckoo song: Midnight!

Merry Christmas. *Fröhliche Weihnachten*.

J ANUARY 15, 1848

Dear Oma,

Thank you for your beautiful Christmas letter. We have read it over and over, loving every word of cheer and hope for the future of your Amerikaners! I hope that you have received my letter about our first Christmas in the new land, our first Christmas without Mama.

Now it is 1848. It is hard to imagine that we have been already in Texas for a whole year, ja? We love it here more each day, and always there are new things to learn and see of this vast country.

This week we had our first visit from a band of Indians, and it was a real experience.

I shall try to describe it to you.

Papa came rushing into the house and told me to load the flintlock, he had seen a band of Indians approaching on ponies. They were still far away, he said, their single-file line a moving ribbon up and down the hills across the river.

As we began to worry for our safety, Jeff came galloping up on Schatzie and pointed to the riders.

"Lipans," he said in a calm voice.

"They will not harm us. They are here to trade buffalo hides with the traders who have come to town. It will be a sight to watch 'em set up their camp and show their wares.

"This band has been here before, once, when my parents and I first came to Industry. They are nomads and carry all their be-

longings with them wherever they wander. If we can find Herr
Ernst, *perhaps he can arrange a meeting with the chief for you,*
Herr *von Scholl."*

*"Ja, Jeff, that would be good," Papa said. "I will ride into
Industry and ask Friedrich right now, if you will stay with Tina
and the children while I am gone. For safety's sake, keep the flintlock loaded and close by.*

*"I know you say there is no danger, Jeff, but there have been
so many stories . . ."*

*Papa's voice trailed off. He did not want to think about the
stories of Indians that he had heard from other settlers.*

He rode into Industry and, later, returned with both Herr *and*
Frau Ernst.

Herr *Ernst greeted us and said, "Louise has come to keep her
namesake, little Louisa, so that you and the boys can accompany
your father and me to visit the Indian encampment. You will like
that, ja?"*

*The boys squealed with delight, and I quickly put on my sec-
ond-best dress and sunbonnet and was ready to go with Papa and*
Herr Ernst. *We took Schatzie's cart to the river and then crossed
on a raft that some of the townspeople had constructed for this
very event.*

*It was almost like an old German town fair, Oma. A festival
atmosphere, with the settlers roaming around looking at the Indians' wares, buffalo skins mostly, and the Indians busily setting
up their camp.*

*That is, the women were setting up camp. The men seemed to
have nothing to do but sit and smoke their pipes and watch the
women do all the work.*

*There is so much to describe to you, I do not know where
to begin.*

*First, the people: as Jeff said, the Lipans are nomads, wander-
ers, and carry very little with them. They probably wear the only
clothing they own and have few household items.*

*The men, their dark bronze skins glowing in the sun, wear
feathered and horned headdresses on their coal-black short hair.
They do not have long braids as in pictures which I have seen.
Their faces are painted with ochre in shades of red, yellow, green*

and black, a sort of geometric design, it is. Very grotesque and frighening it would have been if Herr Ernst and Jeff did not assure us that this is a friendly tribe.

The men and women wear similar clothing of buckskin, skirts and leggings for the women, and breechclouts, a long, hanging panel of wool or buckskin which reaches from the waist to the ground, for the men. Both wear the same type of leggings and moccasins.

Some of the costumes were quite lovely, with fringe cut into the leather or bead work in many colors. Most, however, were ragged and dirty looking.

Everything, everywhere smelled! Of freshly butchered meat and drying buffalo hides—ugh!—and of general squalor. These people seem to me to be very poor, and I could not help but feel sorry for the way they must live and work. Especially, the women. . . .

Several of the squaws were building shelters for the tribe: small, squat tipis, crudely made of brush and stiff, dirty buffalo hides. The women must cut the poles from nearby trees and set them up, then cover them with the hides and brush which they and the little children gather in quantities for their campfires.

Other women were braiding horsehair or cutting narrow strips of horse skin for ropes; others scraped the smelly buffalo skins, using a hooklike, short-handled instrument. A squaw passed us leading a pack horse laden with venison.

All of them worked with a fierce determination in their faces; I did not see one smile during the whole visit.

"Do the women even have to provide the meat for the men, Jeff?" I asked, beginning to feel very angry for these poor squaws. They all looked to be ninety, but must, in fact, be very young women as most of them carried little, black-eyed babies in woven or leather bags strapped to their backs.

"Naw," Jeff answered, grinning, "the men hunt the game. But they leave it where it falls, and the squaws go out and bring it home and prepare it for eatin' or dryin'."

Oma, I must admit that often I get angry at all the work we German women do. But at least, our men are toiling in the fields or building homes, working right beside us. It made me feel very *lucky to be who I am, and not one of those poor Indian women.*

I wandered through the village looking at the people, especially the darling fat babies with their stick-straight, black hair and solemn brown faces. Papa and **Herr** *Ernst, with Jeff and the boys trailing behind them, were inspecting the articles that the Lipans had brought to trade. They would gladly exchange buffalo robes for woolen horse blankets. Animal pelts were going for small amounts of salt or corn. They had ponies, too, mostly wild ones they had captured for trade.*

Papa did not buy anything from the Indians. He did not see the chief, either. A young brave came out of the chief's tipi and said, "Chief sleeps. Come back."

Papa and **Herr** *Ernst decided that Chief Big Owl did not consider them worthy of conversation or of his time.*

We went home then. I, for one, was glad to get back across the river. The Indians had been friendly enough, but it is a strange feeling to be among people whose lives and customs, language and religion are so different from our own.

I think, though, that it was a good thing for all of us, to see this, ja?

Ach, I hear Louisa calling me! She seems to know, always, when it is I sit down for a moment to myself. It is then that she cries. But, mostly, Oma, she is a dear, sweet baby, and I love her with all my heart.

Papa and the boys send their love to you, as I, always, remain
Your loving Granddaughter,
Christina Eudora von Scholl

THE Lipans remained across the river for two weeks, trading with the people of Industry and the up-river traders who had come into town to meet them.

Tina became accustomed to hearing their voices over the half-mile distance between them. She watched an occasional hunting party start off into the woods at the edge of the river, looking for the night's supper. After dark, the lights of their campfires lit up the sky with an orange-amber glow.

Gradually, the von Scholls forgot their initial worry over the Indians and began to take them for granted. Papa continued the one precaution of tying the horses on the far side of the house where he could keep better watch on them.

Tina was too busy to worry about Indians. She had many more chores to do, with Mama gone and Louisa growing so fast. She still tried to help Papa at the school, taking the baby with her in a basket. She wished that she had the hanging bag the Indian squaw used to carry her papoose on her back. It looked far more convenient than lugging a heavy basket around.

On the day that was to change Tina's life, she had more than the usual household work to do. Papa had brought a venison home and she must make jerky, a Texian way of salting and drying meat. Besides milking, churning, feeding Louisa, gathering the few eggs the chickens were generous enough to lay, and cooking the meals, Tina decided to do the laundry.

The weather had been cold, but today was warm and balmy for January with a fresh breeze blowing and blue sky overhead—a perfect day to dry clothes.

She started a fire in the cookstove from logs and branches which the boys had gathered and placed by the back wall of the house for her convenience.

After hoisting the heavy copper wash kettle up onto the stove, she carried water into the house from the barrel the boys must keep filled from the river. While the kettle of water started to heat, she gathered the clothes she would wash and took them and her lye soap outside, behind the house. She would do the laundry while Louisa had her afternoon nap.

It would take about an hour for the water to heat on the wood-burning stove, but Tina did not waste the time. She prepared a hearty lunch for the four males in her domain.

Papa thanked her for the good food and hurried off to town on Schatzie to see if he could find some fencing materials.

Jeff and the boys devoured their meal, eating the cornbread at almost mouth-scorching temperature. Nodding his thanks, Jeff grabbed the flintlock, powderhorn and lead balls.

"Fred and Will and me are goin' to see if we can bag some small game, a rabbit or squirrel, for a tasty supper," he said as they started to leave.

"Before you go," Tina said, "will you carry the kettle to the back yard? Watch, the water is boiling hot."

"No trouble at all, is it, boys?" Jeff said, with a smile for Tina.

That done, they hurried off on their hunting expedition.

Tina was thankful to have the house to herself again. She fed Louisa, burped her and put the chubby baby back into her cradle. Then she rushed out to the back yard to get the washing done while Louisa slept.

With her kitchen knife, Tina sliced some of Mama's lye soap into the steamy water and swished it around. A few suds appeared, then the soap dissolved into a milky liquid. She dropped the clothes into the water, hot and saturated with the strong lye soap. She took an old broom handle and stirred the clothes.

I feel like an old witch, stirring up my magic brew, she thought, grinning. As she worked, she hummed a tune that Oma had taught her when she was a little girl, and daydreamed of a lovely life where there was no laundry to do.

She caught only a fleeting glimpse of the two Indians as they ran from the front of the house, jumped onto their waiting ponies and sped off toward the river. One seemed to be carrying a bundle.

Tina's heart stopped.

Louisa!

She bolted around the corner of the house, trying to see what the fleeing Indian carried in his arms, but unable to make it out.

At the heavy door, which stood half ajar, she stopped, motionless with a ravaging fear, afraid to see what her palpitating heart told her she might find inside the house. All her senses seemed to break down, as though paralyzed. She had difficulty moving, breathing.

A faraway voice inside her stupefied brain said, "You must go in, Tina. You must find out what has happened to Louisa."

Still, she could not move.

Suddenly, as though every part of her body and mind had revitalized itself, Tina went into swift action.

She shoved the heavy door open, sped across the room to Louisa's crib.

Empty.

Throwing herself down beside the little bed, she fumbled with the blankets, as though Louisa might be there, but invisible.

No . . . she was gone!

They had kidnapped her!

A sob tore from Tina's throat.

"Oh, mein Gott . . . Louisa!

No more hesitation . . . no more paralysis of mind or body. A sudden raging anger swept over Tina. They had no right to her little sister! They could not come into someone's home and take a baby from it!

No, she, Tina, would not allow it!

She ran to the corner where the flintlock was kept. Then she remembered that Jeff and the boys had taken it with them. Oh, how she wished she knew where they were now! Or Papa!

Where was Papa? Gone to Industry, on Schatzie. It was up to her to get Louisa back.

What would she do, all alone, to take her baby sister away from the Indians? She must hurry . . . they must not harm Louisa. She must rescue her from them, somehow. And quickly.

But how?

Tina realized suddenly that she had been running around the big room in circles, her breath coming in huge, sobbing gasps, her eyes searching for answers that her mind could not find. Several times she ran back to the cradle. Had she been mistaken? Or dreamed all of this? Would Louisa be there, sleeping peacefully?

No.

She forced herself to stop in mid-stride, take stock of the situation and try to think, to reason.

The Indians, the Lipans, were a friendly tribe, traders, Jeff had insisted. And so they had seemed . . . till now.

Maybe, they would be willing to trade Louisa for something which they would think more valuable than a small girl-baby.

She had to try.

What did she have that the Indians might think worth trading a small child for, even a squaw-child who, at least, could work for them some day? The thought made Tina's soul cringe.

Her frantic eyes roamed the sparsely furnished cabin. They had so little of value. So little that would appeal to an Indian who held all the bargaining power in his arms.

Oh, dear *Gott*, don't let them harm her.

She had to find something. Again, she swept the cabin with her eyes, looking for something, anything. . . .

She had to hurry; her clock's little cuckoo had just announced four-o'clock. She remembered Papa saying at breakfast that the Indians were packing to leave before sunset.

That *was* it!

Her clock!

If she could show Chief Big Owl her little clock and demonstrate its cunning cuckoo . . . maybe, just maybe, he would order the brave who kidnapped Louisa to give her up.

Quickly, without another thought, Tina took the clock down from its place on the wall. Wrapping it in Louisa's blanket, she ran from the house and jumped onto the bare back of her mare, Lisette. No time to saddle her; Tina hoped she could hang on as she urged Lisette to a gallop towards the river. She had never ridden bareback before.

One hand clutched the clock with a fierce, painful grip, so afraid she was that she might drop it and all would be lost. With her other hand entangled in Lisette's brown mane to keep her balance, Tina rode like the wind.

As she had been so many times before, she was grateful that Lisette was her friend. She would help her rescue Louisa. As though she sensed the importance of this trip, the mare boldly entered the river, struggled with the swift current and scrambled up the far bank. Tina held tight, as sheets of icy water rushed over them and then poured back into the river. Lisette gained the far bank.

Tina pulled Lisette to a halt. Now that she was here, in

the Indians' encampment, she was uncertain as to how to proceed. How she wished that Chief Big Owl had seen fit to meet with Papa and *Herr* Ernst when they had requested a visit. She could go to him for help with a little more confidence.

No, she was on her own. It was up to her, Tina, to save Louisa. She must be very careful and do everything just right.

She looked around her. The camp seemed alive with activity. The squaws were dismantling the little community they had lived in but two short weeks, then would set up again at the next stop. Only one tipi remained standing.

Tina supposed that it belonged to Chief Big Owl. Timidly she slid down from Lisette's back and hobbled her. Several of the laboring squaws glanced curiously at this lone white female who had come into their midst.

Tina decided that the only way to handle the situation was to act bravely and boldly. If the Indians guessed how frightened she was, it could be dangerous for both her and Louisa.

With a firm stride, clutching her blanket-covered bundle, she headed toward the lone tipi. How would she make herself understood? Could the chief speak English? No, she remembered *Herr* Ernst saying that he could not, although many of the tribal chieftains spoke it very well.

She stood at the entrance of the tipi, hesitant, wondering how to get the chief's attention.

Then, within the tent, a baby cried.

Louisa.

Tina burst into the tipi, her face a picture of rage, fear and determination. No one would take her baby sister away from her. No one, not even an Indian chief!

Without realizing what she was doing, Tina stood above the chief who sat on a buffalo hide, smoking a long, narrow pipe. Her German, more fluent and more natural to her than English, poured out in an emotional outburst.

The chief gazed up at her in amazement. What was this

white woman-child doing in the tipi of Chief Big Owl? Who had allowed this?

At the puzzled look on the chief's face, Tina realized that she had been speaking in a tongue even more foreign to the Indians than English.

Quickly, before her burst of bravery should abandon her, she cried, "Chief Big Owl, I implore you. Give me back my baby sister. Please. . . ."

As she hesitated, waiting for some sign from the old chief that he had understood her, Tina let her eyes search the large tipi for Louisa.

What had they done with her?

Behind the chief, who, Tina realized now, was very, very old, sat a wrinkled, old woman. She stared at Tina with large, dark eyes, her expression wary and fearful.

Tina wondered why. It was she who should be afraid, if anyone.

Then, she saw Louisa.

Her tiny, blond-haired, pink-cheeked sister lay, uncon-
cerned and content, on the cross-legged lap of this ancient
Indian crone.

There was a stirring from behind her. She recognized
the voice of the young brave who had told Papa and *Herr*
Ernst that "Chief sleeps . . . come back."

He spoke English!

Turning, her eyes wide, she saw the fierce, young Indian moving stealthily and menacingly toward her. Instinctively, she retreated a step.

Then stood her ground. Her natural stubbornness, la-
mented for years by Mama and recognized with respect by
her young brothers, came to Tina's rescue. She would not
be intimidated. She would talk to the chief and try to
strike a bargain with him.

With all the bravado she could muster, she turned to the
young brave and spoke.

"I come to see Chief Big Owl. Will you tell him what I
have to say, please?"

As her knees were about to buckle under her, she gave
the young Indian a large smile. She did not wait for his
reaction, but plunged ahead.

"I would be pleased if the chief would look at what I
have to offer him in place of that unworthy girl-baby."

She pointed to Louisa, indicating that the child wasn't
worth much, but that she was willing to take her off
their hands.

She pulled the blanket from around the little clock. The
time read twenty minutes past four. With her finger, she
advanced the hands to just before five.

"Chief Big Owl," she said firmly and in a friendly manner, "I have a wondrous thing here for you. It is something
to give you and your squaw much happiness. May I show
you how it works?"

As she had hoped, the younger Indian spoke in his Lipan tribal tongue to the chief, gesturing toward Tina and
the clock. The chief peered at Tina through inscrutable

eyes and said nothing. Plainly, he was waiting to see her "wondrous thing."

Glancing to make sure she still had his attention, Tina quickly moved the minute hand on the delicate wooden clock to twelve. Five o'clock.

The tiny door flew open and the bird's cocky head appeared, bobbing up and down. "Cuckoo . . . Cuckoo . . ." Five times. Then back into his house he disappeared, the door closing behind him.

Tina looked at Chief Big Owl.

His expression changed but little. Only his eyes squinted shut a bit, as he sat drawing on his pipe. The squaw squealed a delighted cackle and pointed to the clock.

In turn, Tina pointed to her sister. Looking the chief squarely in the eye, she said, "Swap."

She held out the clock to the chief. Once more she turned the hands, and the dainty bird performed his hourly exhibition.

"Swap," she repeated. She looked at the old woman. She was clutching Louisa tightly to her shrunken bosom. It was clear to Tina that she had no intention of trading the baby for anything, even a noisy little bird.

Tina's heart sank. Was it all hopeless, after all?

No, she told herself. *It is the chief I must convince, not the squaw.*

Holding the clock closer to the chief so that he could hear its ticking, she tried once more.

"Swap."

Point to the clock . . . point to the baby . . . do not show how frightened you are. . . .

The old chief arose from his squatting position, first carefully laying aside his pipe.

Silently, he moved toward Tina, who was holding her breath. He held out his arms and carefully removed Oma's little clock from Tina's grasp.

What would he do now? He was in control here. He could decide to kill her and Louisa, or send her away without baby or clock. . . .

Tina said a quick prayer.

The chief handed the clock to the young brave and spoke a few words. The brave laughed. Then Chief Big Owl bent down and lifted Louisa from the squaw's arms. She said nothing, but Tina saw the pained look on her old, weathered face.

"Here. Take baby. Swap. Chirping bird very good." Chief Big Owl spoke, in hesitant, but understandable, English.

So, he had been able to speak to her all along.

She did not wait for him to change his mind. With a last, longing look at her little clock, she grasped Louisa in her arms, nodded her goodbye to the chief, and walked—as slowly as she could force herself—out of the tipi.

Without looking back, she found Lisette where she had left her. With one hand grasping the horse's mane and the other tightly holding Louisa, she swung herself up onto the mare.

Amidst the curious stares of the Indian villagers, Tina galloped toward the river with her baby sister in her arms.

Tina's heart sang with joy.

Louisa is safe . . . safe. . . .

We are going home.

The ache over the loss of her Oma's clock would come later.

19

TINA never afterward remembered the ride back. She only realized they were safe, she and Louisa, who immediately put up a lusty yell for her goat's milk supper.

As Lisette carried them up the last hill, in sight of the little log house which now meant so much to her, Tina saw Papa, Jeff and the boys, frantically waving their arms.

They must have been so worried, she thought, when they came home and Louisa and I were both missing.

Jeff and Will came racing toward them, not waiting until she reached the house to help Tina dismount. She handed Louisa to Jeff and steadied herself, holding Will's arm. She had a feeling of unreality, as though this past hour had been a dream.

"What happened to you, Tina?" Will's curiosity could wait no longer. "Where have you and Louisa been, and why are you all wet and muddy?"

"*Ach*, Will," Tina said, with a tired sigh. "I will tell everyone all about what has happened, but now. . . ."

"Now," interrupted Jeff, "we will get you to the house for some rest. You are white as a sheet and shaking. After you feel better, you can talk. The boys and I will feed Louisa her bottle, eh, boys?"

Will nodded and Fred, who had just joined them, did likewise. Papa came rushing up to Tina and put his arms about her. "Oh, *Liebchen*, what was it? What happened, while we were away?"

"The Indians . . . kidnapped . . . Louisa. I had to . . . get her back . . . traded . . . my clock . . . my clock. . . ."

Darkness enveloped her as Tina fainted in Papa's arms.

When she awoke, she was in her own bed, covers to her chin, and morning sunlight streaming in the windows. She sat upright, wondering how long it had been since someone had put her there.

Louisa. Where was the baby?

Panic trickled through her veins as she saw the empty cradle. Oh no . . . it couldn't be . . . not again.

Then, from the other end of the big room which served as living, dining, kitchen and bedrooms for all of them, Tina heard giggles, then low laughter.

The boys. Surely, they would not laugh if their tiny sister were kidnapped again.

With great effort she got out of her bed, her long flannel nightgown trailing on the floor, her hair a tangled fright and eyes still sleep-clouded.

Then she saw them. Will and Fred, lying on Papa's bed, had made a circle with their bodies. In the middle of the circle, kicking little feet in the air to the delight of her two big brothers, was Louisa.

Danke, mein Gott.

"Will, Fred!" Tina cried out to them. "What are you two doing, at home, taking care of the little sister, while the big one sleeps and sleeps?"

"Tina, you are awake! I must go call Papa and Jeff. They are outside, milking Daisy and gathering the eggs, while we watch over the princess here, *Ja*?" Will gazed with love at the tiny baby.

"*Ach*, I cannot believe it! Why should everyone take over my work, and I lie here on my back asleep like a winter's bear in the Black Forest of Germany, eh?"

"Ah, my Tina, you are up!" Papa's happy voice sang out as he came bustling into the house, the egg basket in one hand, a full milk pail in the other.

"How is our heroine doing this morning, eh? Let Papa get you something to eat. Are you not starving . . . with no supper last night?"

"*Ach*, Papa." Tina's voice was unsure of itself and quavered a little. "I do not know what happened. All I am sure of is that Louisa and I sailed out of the Indian camp on my dear Lisette—remember how you told me that she would be my best friend someday, just like the real Lisette in Oldenburg? You were so very right, Papa. She behaved like a noble steed, my little Lisette."

Then, shyly, "Where is Jeff?"

Papa grinned, a little teasing grin. "Jeff is finishing the washing that you were too lazy to do yesterday, Tina!" He chuckled at his joke, then became more serious.

"I have never seen anyone so frantic with worry as was Jeff when we came home and found you and Louisa gone.

"Fred, go tell Jeff that the lazy one is awake. Now, Tina, what shall it be for breakfast, eh? Papa is the cook."

Tina sat, an hour later, at the table where she had eaten her full of Papa's meal—an omelet made with the fresh eggs, biscuits with her home-churned butter and, since this was a special breakfast, some of the precious wild grape jelly that Mama had made, and a big mug of Daisy's sweet milk.

She looked about her. Will and Fred sat on either side of her, chins in hands, elbows on table, watching every bite she ate and asking a thousand questions. Papa sat across from her, his eyes full of love and pride. And Jeff, the *Amerikaner* who had become like one of their family, stood next to Papa, meticulously folding Louisa's little clothes, fresh from the clothesline outdoors where he had hung them to dry.

She had told them the whole story as she ate. Their expressions changed with each sentence. Sometimes she saw fear, sometimes anger, then a dawning realization of what she had accomplished single-handedly. Finally, their eyes all held the same emotion: pride.

Her heart overflowed with happiness to see the looks on their faces.

Tina finished her story and her breakfast at the same time. She lifted Louisa from her cradle and gave her a squeeze.

"You know, Papa, I felt sorry for the old squaw. Her eyes had real pain in them, when Chief Big Owl took Louisa from her. But, oh, I am so thankful that the chief wanted Oma's clock in his tipi more than he wanted a little white squaw child!"

"Yes, Daughter, I am thankful, too." Papa suddenly became very busy with clearing Tina's breakfast dishes from the table—an act she had never before seen her father do.

"Ja, thankful that you both are safe, and at home where you belong."

"Yes, Papa," Tina said softly, kissing the baby's soft cheek and staring thoughtfully at the empty spot on the wall where the little cuckoo clock had been.

"Tina," Jeff said with hesitation in his voice, "will you put on your cape and come for a walk with me?" He looked from Tina to Papa to the boys, daring any of them to laugh or tease.

"Yes, Jeff, that sounds like a fine idea. I have eaten too much of Papa's delicious breakfast."

. . . How can I describe what happened next, Oma? When, really, nothing happened. Nothing outward, anyway. We strolled down the path as we had done so many times before, but somehow this time was special. I sensed it in the way Jeff had looked at me back in the house, and how he took my hand now, as we walked along.

I could scarcely breathe. I guess that is normal when a person is in love, is it not, Oma? And I think that, ja, I must be in love with this tall, red-headed American.

And I am convinced that he is in love with me. For he, too, seemed to have difficulty with the breathing.

Ach, I wish he were not so shy, Oma. I feel, almost, that

someday I will have to put the words in his mouth for him, ja? But, there is plenty of time for that.

Now it is enough to know that we are here in America, in Texas, together, with all of our lives before us. Knowing that Jeff will be a part of my future and my life makes my heart sing, Oma.

It helps make up for the loss of my dear clock. I promised to keep it always, I know this, my grandmother. But, I know too, that you are happy with me that it could be the means to get Louisa home with us once more.

In a way, although I will never see it again, my clock is more dear to me than ever. It has become a symbol of two things: first, of your love for me, and next, of my love for Louisa. You can be sure, Oma, that I will always love and stand guard over this little one that our dear Mama has left in my care.

157

I know, too, that I do not need the clock as I once did, Oma. Even without it, I will remember and love you always.

I have learned a valuable lesson, there in Chief Big Owl's tipi, Oma.

Possessions are nothing.

People are everything.

Is it not so, my Oma?

Your loving Granddaughter,
Christina Eudora von Scholl

Glossary

Adelsverein or **Verein**—Society for the Protection of German Immigrants to Texas

Auf Wiedersehen—Goodbye. See you again.

Danke—Thank you

Frau—Mrs.

Gut—good

Herr—Mr.

Ja—yes

Liebchen—dear one

Mein Gott—my God

Nein—no

Nichts—nothing

Pfeffernüsse—German cookies

Schatzie—little sweetheart

Schnaps—a drink

Strudel—a filled pastry

Tannenbaum—Christmas tree

Wienerschnitzel—breaded veal

Wunderbar—wonderful

Suggested Readings

Barlett, John. *The Latin Colony, A Personal Narrative*. Sisterdale, Texas: 1850.

Benjamin, Gilbert Giddings. *The Germans in Texas*. Austin,
Texas: Jenkins Publishing Co., 1974.

Berlitz, Charles. *German, Step by Step*. New York: Everest
House, 1979.

Emigrant. *The Far Western Frontier—Texas in 1840*. New
York: Arno Press, 1973.

Encyclopedia Britannica, Vol. 10., pps. 262–263. Chicago:
William Benton, Publisher, 1959.

Flach, Vera. *A Yankee in German America—Texas Hill Country*. San Antonio, Texas: The Naylor Co., 1973.

Geiser, Samuel Wood. *Naturalists of the Frontier*. Texas:
Southern Methodist University, 1948.

Geue, Ethel Hander. *New Home in a New Land—German
Immigration to Texas, 1847–1861*. Waco, Texas: Waco
Press, 1970.

———— and Chester W. Geue, Ed. *A New Land Beckoned—
German Immigration to Texas, 1844–1847*. Waco, Texas:
Texian Press, 1974.

Haskew, Corrie Pattison. *Historical Records of Austin and
Waller Counties*. Houston, Texas: Premier Printing, 1969.

Holman, David, Comp. *Hard Times in Texas, 1840—1890*.
Austin, Texas: Roger Beacham, Pub., 1974.

Institute of Texan Cultures. *Texians and the Texans*. San Antonio, Texas: University of Texas at San Antonio, n.d.

————. *The German Texans*. San Antonio, Texas: University
of Texas at San Antonio, 1970.

Jenkins, John Holland. *Recollections of Early Texas*. Austin, Texas: University of Texas Press, 1958.

Jordan, Gilbert J. *German Texana*. Burnet, Texas: Eakin Press, 1980.

————. *Yesterday in the Hill Country*. College Station, Texas: Texas A & M Press, 1979.

Jordan, Terry G. *German Seed in Texas Soil*. Austin, Texas: University of Texas Press, 1966.

Kreuger, Max Amadeus Paulus. *Second Fatherland*. College Station, Texas: Texas A & M Press, 1976.

Lester & Kerr. *Historic Costume*. Peoria, Illinois: Charles A. Bennett Co., Inc., 1977.

Lich, Glen E. and Reeves, Dona B., Ed. *German Culture in Texas—a Free Earth*. Boston: Twayne Pub., 1980.

Metcalf, Edna, Comp. *The Tree of Christmas*. Nashville, Tennessee: Abingdon Press, 1979.

Monken, Bernard. Untitled Article. Boerne, Texas: Frontier Times, February, 1927.

Moore, Francis, Jr. *Map and Description of Texas, 1840*. Waco, Texas: Texian Press, 1965.

Olmstead, Frederick Law. *Journey through Texas*. Austin, Texas: von Boeckmann-Jones Press, 1962.

Parents' Magazine. *Christmas Holiday Book*. New York: Parents' Magazine Press, 1972.

Pickrell, Annie Doom. *Pioneer Women in Texas*. Austin, Texas: Jenkins Pub. Co., 1970.

Pool, William C. *A Historical Atlas of Texas*. Austin, Texas: The Encino Press, 1975.

Roemer, Dr. Ferdinand. *Texas—with Particular Reference to German Immigration and the Physical Appearance of the Country*. San Antonio, Texas: Standard Printing Co., 1935.

Ragsdale, Crystal Sasse. *The Golden Free Land*. Austin, Texas: Landmark Press, 1976.

Schmidt, Curt E. *Oma & Opa—German-Texan Pioneers*. San Antonio, Texas: Accurate Litho & Printing Co., 1975.

Sibley, Marilyn McAdams. *Travelers in Texas, 1761—1860*. Austin: University of Texas Press, 1967.

Smith, Ashbel. *Reminiscences of the Texas Republic*. Austin, Texas: The Pemberton Press (Brasada Reprint Series), 1967.

Syers, William Edward. *Off the Beaten Trail*. Waco, Texas: Texian Press, 1979.

Wernecke, Herbert H. *Christmas Customs Around the World*. Philadelphia: The Westminster Press, 1959.

Wilcox, R. Turner. *The Mode in Costume*. New York & London: Charles Scribner's Sons, 1958.

About the Author

RAISED in Idaho and Indiana, Marj Gurasich has been a resident of the Houston area for over thirty years. She is the author of several nonfiction studies and the juvenile novel, *Red Wagons and White Canvas*.

The inspiration for *Letters to Oma* was twofold: While researching the history of Industry, Texas, for an article on the 150th anniversary of town founder Friedrich Ernst's arrival in Texas, she came across a magazine photograph of an antique German cuckoo clock. She had long been fascinated by the story of the German settlers, their hardships and sacrifices, and their immense contributions to the patchwork-quilt culture that is Texas. The clock inspired her to create a story about those early settlers, the story of Christina and her family . . . and her clock.

Typesetting by G&S

Printing and binding by THOMSON-SHORE

Design and illustration by WHITEHEAD & WHITEHEAD